WRITTEN BY DAYLIGHT

Written by Daylight

by

John Howard

Swan River Press
Dublin, Ireland
MMXXIV

Written by Daylight
by John Howard

Published by
Swan River Press
at Æon House
Dublin, Ireland
June MMXXIV

www.swanriverpress.ie
brian@swanriverpress.ie

Stories © John Howard
This edition © Swan River Press

Cover design by Meggan Kehrli from
"Man Sleeping in L.A. Apartment" (2011)
by Eoin Llewellyn

Set in Garamond by Steve J. Shaw

Paperback Edition
ISBN 978-1-78380-772-7

Swan River Press published
a limited hardback edition of
Written by Daylight in June 2013.

Contents

"Where Once I Did My Love Beguile"

Without realising it, Stephen Langley was about to undergo an experience that would change his life forever.

He was five years old. Stephen was at school, walking around the playing-field on a warm spring day. He ambled along, next to the wire fence that separated the field from the back gardens of the houses of Chapel Street. He was running his hand along the rusting diamond-shaped links, looking every now and then at the brown stains growing on his small fingers.

Suddenly he stopped, his self-absorption ended by seeing something glinting, out of the corner of an eye. He looked through the fence, gripping it now with both hands. Flakes of rust fell away, through his fingers into the grass.

On the other side of the fence, sitting on a battered chair in his garden, was an old man. He took his cap off and wiped his forehead. He had been weeding and was hot. He unbuttoned another button on his collarless shirt and fanned his leathery face with his other hand. And in his waistcoat there hung a bright watch-chain that caught the sun and glittered into the eye of the small boy now gazing through the fence.

Stephen was still gripping the fence with both hands. It rattled slightly. The man in his garden looked up and saw him.

"Hello," he said, smiling.

"Hello," said Stephen. Then he released the fence and pointed at the man's waistcoat. "What's that?" he asked.

"This?" he said. "It's my watch-chain. Now look."

He took the watch itself out, slowly, and popped it open. He got up and walked over to the fence, showing its face to the boy.

Stephen looked at it intently. His eyes narrowed into slits as he gazed at it. "That's not the time," he said after a while, as if the man was trying to trick him.

The man laughed. "No, you're right there, boy," he said. "Watch's busted. Too old. A bit like me. You like it?"

The gold caught the sun again, glinting in the boy's face. Stephen's eyes lit up, with more than the yellow light, and he tried to put his hand through the links of the fence. Perhaps he thought that the old man would give him the shining watch, with its pent-up time.

The boy still looked happy, even though he must have realised that he wasn't going to get the watch. He looked at the man. "*You're* not busted," he said. "You do all that in your garden. Can I hold it?"

"It won't fit through the fence," the man replied. For a moment he thought that the boy was going to cry. "Tell you what, boy," he said. "If your Mum doesn't mind, you can come round here after school tomorrow and see it. You can hold it if you like. How's that?"

Just then a teacher started ringing the hand bell to show that the lunchtime break was over. Stephen turned and began to run back to school. But he was grinning, and shouted "Thank you! Thank you!" as he ran away.

That was how Stephen Langley met Stan Lacey, and how the course of Stephen's life changed forever.

The next afternoon Stan was working in his front garden. It was tiny, almost too small to turn round in, but it faced Chapel Street, and the children had to pass it on their way home after school.

Stan was often lonely, since his wife Edith had died two years before. He was retired from his job at Collier's, the furniture factory at the top of the street, and spent most of his time gardening, or sitting in his front room drinking tea and looking at the photos on his mantelpiece. Now seventy, he looked forward to the change of a visit. He and his wife had had no children of their own.

Stan sat on the low front wall of his garden. Now children walked and ran past, shouting and screaming. Mothers pushed prams and walked in small groups down the street.

"Hello!"

Stan turned round as he heard the small voice and felt a tapping low down on his back. The boy was standing there in the street, a shy grin on his face like before.

"Hello, boy," Stan said.

"Can I see it? Can I?" Stephen held out his hand.

"Hold on, hold on!" Stan said, laughing. He put his hand on the wall next to him. "Sit up here."

Stephen scrambled up. "Please?" he said.

"Does your mother know you're here? Where do you live?"

Stephen looked serious for a moment. He nodded. "I live at 95 Willoughby Way," he recited.

"That's one of the new houses," Stan said. "Well, and what's your name, boy?"

"Stephen Langley."

"That's a good Littleworth Green name," Stan said.

He found out later that Stephen was related to the Langleys who ran the hardware shop in the High Street, and that he had moved to Littleworth Green after his father had died in an accident.

Stephen said, "You're Mr. Lacey." As if he was daring Stan to deny it. "Miss Stretton said."

"Did she say what my first name is?"

He thought for a moment. "No."

"Shall I tell you?"

"Yes, please!"

"Well, it begins with S, then a T—"

"Stephen!"

"No, it's Stanley. You can call me Stan. Everyone does."

"Can I see that watch now?" Stephen said.

Stan laughed. His face creased up. "That's what you're here for, isn't it, boy?"

He took the watch out of his waistcoat pocket and dangled it in front of Stephen's eyes. Then he opened it.

Stephen reached out and touched the glass gently. "It's still all wrong," he said.

"It's busted," Stan said. "Look how old it is." He showed the boy the engraving on the inside of the lid. *Reginald Lacey from His Father 26 February 1887.* "Nearly eighty years ago," Stan said. "That was *my* dad. Given to him by his father. That watch was old then, as well. I got it from my father when I joined Kitchener's lot. Surprised it lasted as long as it did. Hasn't told the time since the Silver Jubilee. But I like to wear it."

Stephen touched the watch again, as Stan held it in front of him. It turned slowly on its chain. It looked as if it was hypnotising the boy. Then he gazed at Stan, who knew what Stephen wanted. He lowered the watch into Stephen's outstretched hands. The boy cupped them around the watch, as if it was going to escape him.

"Wow," Stephen said under his breath. Then he looked up at Stan again. "Maybe if I hold it long enough tomorrow won't come and school won't come and I can stay home and play or come and help you." His words tumbled out in a rush.

Stan laughed. "But then it'll never be Christmas or holidays or your birthday!"

Stephen's forehead screwed up. "Oh. Don't like birthdays much, anyway."

He held the watch out to Stan, who snapped it shut and slipped it away, back in his waistcoat pocket. "Gone," he said. "But you can see it again, if you like."

"Stan, if the watch went backwards I could get to before when things went bad until it stopped again."

"You'll have to ask your mother or teacher that one," Stan said. "Anyway, you'd better get on home, boy. Look at the clock when you get in. See what time it is."

"I can tell the time," Stephen said proudly.

"I know you can!"

"Thank you for letting me see the watch. See you tomorrow!" He jumped off the wall and ran on down Chapel Street, and round the corner past the pub.

The next afternoon Stan was sitting in his front room, reading the paper. He heard the children coming out of school. Then there was a knock on the front door.

Answering it, Stan saw Stephen standing there, together with his mother. "Afternoon," he said. He looked down at Stephen. "Hello, young man."

Mrs. Langley smiled back, looking a bit harassed. "I hope you don't mind me coming round with Stephen," she said. "He told me that he'd seen you yesterday, and I just wanted to make sure that he wasn't being a nuisance."

Stan rubbed his jaw. He hadn't bothered to shave that morning. Since his wife had died he didn't always bother.

"He wasn't a nuisance. He just wanted to look at my old watch. He's a fine lad, I reckon."

She smiled awkwardly. "Yes, last night I couldn't stop him going on about it. I think he wants to be a time traveller when he grows up!" She laughed. "But as long as you don't mind . . . "

Stephen started to pull on his mother's hand. "Ask him, ask him," he said.

"Mr. Lacey," she said, "would you mind if he came to see you some more, sometimes? His father died last year, and I have my hands so full sometimes. He'd really like to help in your garden. I don't have the time at home . . . And he really liked looking at your watch. It fascinated him."

Stephen looked up at Stan, while he held on to his mother's hand. "Just after school sometimes, Stan," he said.

"Stephen!"

"He said I could call him that. It's his name."

Stan nodded. "It's all right."

"Can I come? Can I? You said I could!"

Stan thought for a moment. "Of course you can, boy. You can help me in the garden, and I've got a few other things you might be interested in."

"Thank you, Mr. Lacey," Mrs. Langley said. "I'm really grateful. He won't be any problem. He's a good boy."

Stephen pointed at Stan's waistcoat, where the watch-chain hung. He smiled up at his mother, pulling at her hand. Stan took the watch out and opened it, lowering it to the level of Stephen's eyes. Stephen touched the glass reverently, and gazed at the frozen hands for a long and inscrutable moment.

Already his life was changing.

Over the next two or three years Stephen visited Stan at least once a week, usually after school. Usually he helped out in the garden, and nearly always asked to look at the watch.

Once Stephen's class did a project on the forthcoming centenary of the school, and Stephen asked Stan if he could see any old photos. Stan showed him his photos, papers, and medals from the First World War. Stephen gazed at them intently, shuffling them and holding them gently. As if they were his vital windows into another time.

One warm afternoon Stephen knocked on Stan's front door after school. "Stan, Stan," he said. "On Sunday we went to West Wycombe and we went up the Golden Ball and had some ice cream, and then we went into some Caves. It was great!"

"You went to the Hellfire Caves? Let's see, I haven't been there since they were opened up again, oh, ten years ago, maybe a bit more . . . "

Stan had always known about the Caves. As a child he and other Littleworth Green boys walked over to West Wycombe for church outings and fights with the West Wycombe boys.

As a lad the ruined and boarded-up entrance had always fascinated Stan. Once he had talked about getting into the Caves, and even made friends with some of the West Wycombe boys who were going to break in and explore. But the lads changed their minds, and Lord Desborough had the boards strengthened and padlocked.

Stan had first met his wife at a social in West Wycombe, when she was in service at the House. Edith had never talked about the Caves. Apart from a few of the local boys, no-one in the village ever mentioned them, and certainly not to outsiders. The villagers didn't hate the Caves, they just ignored them, and preferred it that way. As if West Wycombe Hill's interior darkness was boarded up and kept at bay by a wall of silence and forgetfulness. Over the years, Stan had all but forgotten about the Caves as well.

In the early 1950s, the new Lord Desborough had woken up to the commercial potential of the Hellfire Caves. He had a proper door fitted to the entrance, and parties of visitors went down, provided with candles and miners' helmets.

Stan never thought about his one secret trip down the Caves until Stephen's visit. He remembered the Caves as being chilly and damp, with nothing to see except for the flickering of candles on the rough chalk walls.

"It was really brilliant, Stan," Stephen was saying. "It was like a place where there are ghosts and things. I got chalk all over my arm. It was all wet and cold. I ran away from Mum, but I didn't get lost!"

"It was just dark and dirty when I went there. Did you have proper lamps?"

"There's 'lectric lights. And they've got talking statues all lit up and dressed like in the olden days. And Lord Desborough—"

"Hmmm. Sounds like you had an interesting time. Maybe I'll get back down there one day."

Stephen said, still excited, "I'm going back there lots!"

They went into the back garden and began work.

When he was eleven, Stephen went to Faulkner Road Secondary School. He was no longer able to walk past Stan's house on his way to and from school, or to talk to him through the fence. But he still visited Stan and helped him, talked and listened.

One afternoon Stephen came round after school and showed Stan a pamphlet about the Hellfire Caves. He said that he'd been there with some friends from school. His mother had given him ten New Pence to spend, and he'd bought the booklet.

Stephen talked on about the Caves, like he was a little boy again. He was enthralled by the map of the Caves in the back of the booklet. It was as if he had been given a secret plan, a map to a genuine treasure trove, an exclusive document in order to discover great secrets that no-one else had ever been able to. He traced the passages with his finger. "We walked all the way down there—to the River Styx and back," he said. "We ran around the Catacombs. I got out first. I remembered it all."

Stan looked at the map. It was one long black line with several curves and corners, dead-end passages and returns, thick pillars and circular rooms carved out of the solid chalk. The cover of the pamphlet showed one of the model groups in the Caves—the first Lord Desborough showing his old crony Benjamin Franklin around.

Stan was a bit bewildered by Stephen's sudden interest in what he remembered as a long, dark filthy hole in the ground. But he saw Stephen as the excited little boy after his first visit to an unusual place, and he shook his head and smiled.

"They're great," Stephen said. "I really like going down the Caves. I can't wait to go again. I can go there every Sunday if I use my pocket money."

Over the next couple of years Stan's arthritis slowly got worse, and Stephen did more and more of the actual work in the garden, while Stan sat down and told him what to do, or listened to Stephen talking about school, his friends, life at home.

When he was fourteen, and now taller than Stan, Stephen announced that he wanted to be known as Steve. Stan told him that he only became known as Stan when he began work at Collier's, and that his parents had always called him Stanley.

One day the following year Steve was sitting in Stan's front room drinking tea, when he got out his Hellfire Caves booklet. By then it was getting well worn, tattered and taped on the edges. He had read it over and over again.

He held the booklet out to Stan. "I've been looking at this," he said. "Have you ever heard of it? Do you remember it?" Steve pointed at the open page. "The rhyme, there."

> Take twenty steps and rest awhile;
> Then take a pick and find the stile
> Where once I did my love beguile.
>
> 'Twas twenty-two in Desboro's time,
> Perhaps to hide this cell divine
> Where lay my love in peace sublime.

Stan read the rhyme through. He couldn't make anything of it.

"Never heard of it, boy," he said. "I don't understand it."

Steve looked disappointed. "I thought you might know about it," he said. "What with you knowing about lots of old local things, and your wife coming from West Wycombe."

Stan thought. Edith had never mentioned or repeated the rhyme to him, any more than anyone else from West Wycombe ever had, even though the booklet said that it was an ancient village rhyme.

Steve pointed at the open page again. "There," he said. "How can you have a stile in a cave, anyway?"

"I don't know. I told you I couldn't make it out."

"It must be the key to a secret passage or something. Look at this bit, on the next page. It's another poem. About a secret room in the Caves. It says 'Under the Temple' so that must be the church, I suppose. There must be a secret room down there. It'd be great to find it!"

He showed Stan the other poem. "I don't know," he said. "It still doesn't make much sense to me."

Steve closed the booklet. For a moment he looked like the little boy that Stan first showed his watch to. Like he had a bright future, something to fill his life, give it purpose.

"Stan, I'm going to find that secret room."

Perhaps Stan didn't seem to take Steve seriously enough. "The best of luck to you, boy," he said.

Steve spoke fiercely. "I *will* find it. I'm going to learn all I can about the Caves. Start again now, get interested again, like when I was a kid. Except better!"

The next afternoon Steve and Stan were sitting in the cool front room, resting after working at laying turf.

Steve said, "I asked my English teacher about the rhyme. I showed it to him. He said that a stile can also mean part of a door. So it's not like a stile you have to get over on a path. There must be a secret door down there. In the booklet it mentioned workmen feeling breezes when they were restoring the Caves. I'm going down there on Saturday. And Sunday."

Stan nodded. By now he wasn't at all sure that he understood Steve at all. He remembered that when he had been Steve's age he had already started work. He poured more tea and changed the subject.

"What are you going to do when you leave school, then?" he asked.

Steve shrugged his shoulders. "You have to be sixteen now. I've got all my exams yet. I don't know. Anything, I suppose . . . There's Mum as well."

Stan recalled that he hadn't seen Mrs. Langley around the High Street recently. "How is she?" he asked.

Steve shrugged again. "I don't know. Oh, she's fine. Really great. There's this new bloke around. It's serious this time. He's called Brian. She goes out with him most evenings. Last night she was talking about moving away from Littleworth Green. I don't want to move away. I like it here."

"Maybe she won't want to move far," Stan said. "Just to somewhere else round Wycombe."

"Stan, I don't know at all," Steve said. "Brian's okay, and I'm pleased Mum's got someone, but I don't want it to change things. I want to stay around here."

Stan was at a loss for words. He didn't want to sound insincere. "Things will turn out all right," he said eventually. "They have a way of doing that."

Stan decided to change the subject yet again. "So, boy," he said. "When are you going to get yourself a young lady? When I was your age—"

Steve blushed. Then he looked rather pleased, as if he'd been affirmed or been asked to join a special club. Stan realised that Steve had been looking smarter recently. And today he was wearing new trousers.

"Don't know," he replied.

"Got your eye on anyone then?"

"Not sure. Maybe." Then he got up. "Better be going now, Stan," he said. "I'll help you finish on Monday. I'm going down the Caves Saturday and Sunday."

Steve came round after school on Monday as he'd promised. As they drank their tea, Steve produced a book from his jacket pocket. "Look what I got on Saturday," he said.

He handed Stan the book. He looked at the cover. It was bright, like a horror poster, and showed a large skull with some ruins.

"It's all about the history of the Hellfire Club," Steve said. "It's superb. I've been up late reading it. It's got all about the Caves and what went on. It's got the rhymes as well. Look."

He showed Stan the pages. Stan didn't think that there was much more explanation than in the booklet. But Steve was as taken with it all as ever.

"It'll keep you busy," Stan said as he gave the book back. "It looks odd to me. I bet most of it's made up."

"The secret passage stuff can't be," Steve said earnestly. "I'm sure I felt a breeze down there yesterday. Near the carving, the XXII the rhyme says about. You can't miss that. There must be a secret room or something, where the Club members did all their really special, you know, things. And I'm going to find it!"

"Hmm. You sure you're not courting?" Stan said.

Suddenly Steve grinned. "Well, okay, there's this girl in my class . . . "

"What's her name?"

"Karen."

"Is she fair or dark?"

"She's got dark hair."

Stan smiled. "Well, just you watch it, boy. And all this Caves lark."

He didn't want to get Steve worked up too much. But it made Stan realise how quickly time was going. It seemed to him only yesterday that a little boy had stood at the school fence, looking at his old watch as if all his world depended on it. Now he was growing up fast.

Over the next few weeks Steve visited Stan once a week. But instead of working he just sat drinking tea, talking. He sat in his usual armchair opposite Stan and talked, sometimes in such an intense monotone that Stan thought that Steve was talking in a trance. Or he got excited, and would talk fast, as if he had the need to convince Stan that his experiences and impressions of the Caves were wholly true, but yet open to doubt or needing confirmation by a certain time.

"I go down there as often as I can," he would say. "I take the map and check it all out. I pace the distances and stand still so I can feel any air-currents from secret openings. I have to make sure no-one can see me.

"It's like being inside something alive. The passages are all cool and glistening, and the rooms are like stomachs and things. Spending lots of time down there makes me think of being inside a sort of living body, like in blood vessels or intestines or something. I have to make sure I don't slip over on the slopes or trip over if I'm looking at something.

"I wish they'd get rid of the models and Lord Desborough's commentary. I'd really like to see the Caves all dark and silent, like you used to be able to. Maybe I could ask Lord Desborough, show him all my work. Maybe Mr. Lloyd from school would help . . . Or I could hide down there at closing time . . .

"Right at the bottom of the Caves I can almost feel the weight of the Hill, as if it could all crash in at any minute. But I know it won't. Not on me. The Caves are like sort of holding their breath when I'm there. Like they know me, like I know every bit of them they've shown me so far."

Stan sometimes felt worried about Steve's obsession with the Caves, especially now. But Steve also said that things were going well with Karen too, so Stan thought that she must be keeping Steve in balance.

One afternoon Stan and Steve were raking up grass in the back garden. Steve said, "Stan, when did you first, well, you know, do . . . "

Stan was shocked. This was a different Steve. "Mind your own business," he snapped. He muttered under his breath as he watched Steve raking up the cut grass.

"I can't wait," Steve said, as he continued working. It didn't seem to matter to him whether or not Stan was listening. "All my mates reckon they're up to it," Steve carried on. "But I know it's what the Caves are *really* all about. It's all in the map. I never took any notice until I started going out with Karen. It says in the Hellfire Club book. The Caves are shaped like a woman, you know, like a woman's—"

"Why are you going on like this?" Stan said. "You lads should watch it."

"The map showed me. How to make everything good again and okay in the future. Like having it off with a girl."

Stan thought that he shouldn't really be shocked by Steve. Stan had never been a prude. He hadn't only gone out to work when he'd been Steve's age. But his father would've belted him for talking like that at home, wage-earner though he'd been. But Steve just went on talking.

"They're all doing it," he said. "It's right, me going down the Caves. It'll make things great."

Stan said, "I don't understand what you're going on about. If you want to stay here, then clean your mouth out!"

Steve threw the rake down and went out through the house. Stan heard the front door being slammed.

A week or so later, Stan was coming out of the Mason's Arms after a lunchtime pint. He went over to the High Street Stores to buy some bread. On his way out he met Steve. He had a girl with him.

"Hello, Stan," Steve said.

"Afternoon, young man."

"Are you okay?"

"I'm all right. Come round if you like. You know where I live. Nothing's changed."

The girl said, "Steve . . . ?"

"Oh, this is Mr. Lacey, er, Stan. I've told you about him." He looked at Stan. "Meet Karen."

Stan thought that she was certainly very pretty, like Edith was when they'd first met. "Pleased to meet you," he said, putting out his hand.

They laughed and carried on walking towards the Common. "See you around," Steve said, over his shoulder.

The next week Steve started coming round again.

It was late on a Saturday night in the autumn. Stan was sitting in his front room, thinking about switching his TV off. Suddenly there was a banging on the front door. When he opened it, Steve was standing there. He looked in a state. He had been smartly dressed, but now his trousers were torn, and his elbows and hands were cut and dirty, as if he'd fallen over and been crawling. He had clearly been crying as well.

Stan let him in and sat him down in his usual place.

"It's no good, Stan," Steve wailed. "It's Karen. She's chucked me. We went to this party and she told me that she wanted to be just friends now, and she went off. There were lots of tins of lager and some wine so I had some. And before I went out Mum said that Brian's asked her to marry him and she's going to say yes. I was happy until she said we'd all move from Littleworth Green and I don't want to . . ."

He really started to cry then, wrenching sobs that shook his entire body.

Stan went and got Steve a damp towel so he could clean himself up. "There, there," he said, over and over again. Eventually Steve calmed down.

"What can I do, Stan? You must've had girlfriends before you got married and all that."

In spite of the situation Stan smiled. "Well, yes, I did. And they sometimes gave me the push as well, and I played the field a bit. You're young. You've plenty of time yet."

That seemed to galvanise Steve. Then he said, "But I loved her."

"You'll get over it, boy."

"I'm going back down the Caves again. I've got to. I can do it this time. I can think right this time down there. Things'll start to be okay. Everything. I know they will."

"What do you mean now?"

"It's all in my Hellfire Club book. The one I showed you. Like I said. And the map. It explains it all. The Inner Temple is the end, where it all begins, like in a womb." He pulled a torn piece of paper out of his pocket. "I always have it," Steve said.

Stan took the map reluctantly. He remembered the one from the Caves booklet. The passage curved under West Wycombe Hill, inwards and downwards. The triangular passages before the River Styx and Inner Temple were obvious in their symbolism. Stan thought, not for the first time, that the first Lord Desborough and his Hellfire Club had certainly been a strange bunch of characters.

"It mightn't mean anything," Stan said.

"It does! It must! I've marked it all!" Steve said.

"Everything'll be okay for me if I get down there again. It'll be good with Mum and Brian and I can stay where I want to be. Things'll be like when I was a kid and you showed me your watch and you talked about your medals and things. I know I can find the stile and secret stuff, and get to the heart . . . "

A few minutes later, Steve left, having apologised for causing a fuss. Stan went to bed. He noticed that his watch wasn't on the mantelpiece, but thought that he must have left it somewhere else. He didn't think about it again until he was forced to.

On Sunday Mrs. Langley came round and asked Stan if he'd seen Steve. He said that he hadn't. After she had gone back home to phone the police, Stan sat down in his front room. He felt for his watch-chain, and then remembered that he hadn't seen the watch since the previous day. He searched, but couldn't find it anywhere in the small house.

On Monday afternoon Stan walked to the phone box by the Post Office in the High Street, and, for the first time in his life, called a taxi. The driver took him by the circling road to the graveyard at the top of West Wycombe Hill. "Collect me from the entrance to the Caves in an hour," Stan told the driver.

Stan had never been to look at his wife's grave, but now it seemed right to. He had not been to the Hill since the funeral. He found the grave, and stood in front of it, apparently praying in the warm October sun. Then he turned away, to walk down the Hill, down the long clear slope in front of the Desborough Mausoleum, where he'd played football during the reign of King Edward VII, and when the Caves had been boarded up, secure and ignored.

Walking slowly, Stan arrived at the entrance to the Caves. It had been rebuilt, the ruined gothic arches completed again. There was a café and shop just outside the entrance itself, which was still like a dark wound, slit into the hillside.

Stan sat down in the café and ordered a cup of tea.

"Are you going down the Caves?" the assistant asked.

"No, I don't think so," Stan replied. "I'm a bit shaky on the pins . . . " He laughed.

The assistant started to tidy the counter. Before he turned away, Stan said, "Did you get many visitors yesterday?"

"Oh yes, lots. When it gets like that you've always got to be so careful about not locking anyone in. The little kids are the worst. They think it's fun to try and hide down there."

"No-one tried it on, then?"

"No. But there was some lost property. We found this, down in the Inner Temple. You know, right as far in as you can go."

She reached under the counter and pulled out an old-fashioned watch on a chain. "This must be valuable," she said. "I suppose I'd better let Lord Desborough know." It swung, hypnotically, in the sun streaming in through the window. "It's very old, but it's still working."

Westenstrand

There can never be a true map of Westenstrand. The island's outline constantly changes. Day by day the tides and currents of the North Sea cut away at the sand of its beaches and dunes, shifting it to another place or sweeping it away entirely. The inhabitants are used to the land beneath their feet being changed, disappearing and reappearing, being transformed from one state to another, from solid to liquid or to something involving both. And a particularly severe storm will, very likely, leave behind it not only a host of damaged lives, but wrecked houses, uprooted trees, and boats ripped from their moorings and washed out to sea. An entire beach of Westenstrand's renowned golden sand could advance fifty metres in width or be transformed into a new salt marsh. In the morning, light dawns on an altered world, and another map must be painstakingly put together.

I had hoped that Margit and I would spend the summer vacation together in Munich. It's an expensive and crowded city at the best of times, and even more so in summer, but we had been able to arrange jobs in a restaurant and decided that we could manage on the few marks per week wages until our families could send more money in the autumn.

There had been a note waiting for me in my room. Margit confessed that she'd been growing more worried about some of my friends—or, rather, their influence on me. I knew whom she meant and what. But the result had been that Margit wanted to get away from Munich— and me—for the summer. And she had chosen the far end of the country for her destination.

So when I found that Margit had thrown away our carefully made plans to go to an island called Westenstrand to plant marram grass, I wandered around my room in a state of shock until Armin and Joseph took me out to drink beer in one of the places we frequented and tried to interest me in going along to a public meeting held by the National Socialists. That sobered me, and I saw again what it was Margit was concerned about; but I didn't understand how running away would solve anything. Sure, after a few beers I would talk about the need to reform the Republic—I truly believed that—but as for the methods advocated by the parties led by Hitler or Thälmann, that was another matter, and I was as bothered about them as Margit had finally revealed she really was. I realised that I should've made myself clearer to her.

Margit's action seemed clear enough, though. Perhaps she didn't intend to return, or simply wanted to end things between us, but hadn't wanted to say so to my face. Nevertheless I was still anxious about her—and, certainly, us—and decided that I had to do something about it. I had never heard of Westenstrand. I had never even seen the sea. The largest body of water I knew was the Chiemsee. But none of that stopped me from following Margit as soon as I could. A visit to the University Library filled in some details. I learned that Westenstrand was a long smear of land, flat and scarcely rising above sea level, a few kilometres off the coast just below the border with

Denmark. Joseph told me that he'd been taken on holiday to Westenstrand as a child.

"At least it's still a part of the Reich," Joseph said indignantly. "Unless our current wretched Republic has decided to give it away to Denmark, like they did with northern Schleswig."

"There was a plebiscite," I replied mildly. "The majority who lived there were Danes and opted to join Denmark. It means those who are left within the Reich truly want to be a part of it. I would've thought you'd agree with that."

"That girl did get to you, Peter," Joseph said.

I glared at him over my beer tankard.

"All right then," Joseph continued. "The main town is called Westerdorf. It's surrounded by sand dunes and grass. There's nothing to look at but the sea and the clouds. The only thing that breaks the horizon is the lighthouse, to the north of the town." Joseph said that the scheme Margit had gone to work on in Westenstrand sounded like the compulsory work service schemes that the National Socialists were talking of making students volunteer for when they came into power. That made me all the more anxious. "Let her plant marram grass and help heap up sand against wooden palisades," Joseph went on. "She's doing some good. And she'll be back when it suits her, and not before. If that won't suit you also, Peter, then I'm sorry, but you'll have found out where you stand with her."

"What's the easiest way for me to get there? To this island?"

As just about everybody but me had probably known, Westenstrand was actually no longer an island. A causeway with a railway line had been finished a few years ago and opened by President Ebert himself, just before his death. The connection by rail made thoughts of the journey much less daunting: I wouldn't have to go on a boat after all. By hitch-hiking I got myself to Flensburg. I had scraped some money together before leaving Munich, and had enough to pay for a train ticket to get me from Flensburg to Westerdorf, cross-country across the narrow neck of Schleswig-Holstein. That part of the journey necessitated several changes of train. For the final part of the complex route I sat opposite a strongly-built elderly gentleman with a tanned face and tufts of thick sandy hair sticking out from under his cap. He turned fierce eyes on me for a moment, and then gazed out of the carriage window.

I thought he looked more like a native than a visitor. I leaned across and asked him if he knew where the students were at work planting marram grass.

"First time on the Island?" he asked. I could perceive the capital letter in his tone. It was obvious that for him there was only the one possible island. I smiled and nodded.

"What's so funny?"

"Well, it's just that Westenstrand isn't, ah, an island any more, is it?

My companion turned the full force of his gaze on me. He jabbed at the air in front of my face. "Young man, you're exactly right. Not so long ago any Islander who couldn't handle a boat had to get someone to do it for him, or stay at home. I'm too arthritic to sail now, but I did up until about 1930. I can tell you, though, I wouldn't miss this Ebertdamm if it were swept away with the next great storm tide! I would stay at home and be done with it. But ten minutes by train or ten kilometres by boat, the result's all the same now. The Island is becoming like anywhere else. I don't know why they bother trying to defend it. If the sea wants an island here there'll be one, no matter what shape it is or if anyone's on it."

I tracked Margit down to a bare room in a terrace of unfinished guesthouses and tourist cabins on the north side of Westerdorf. She didn't welcome me with open arms, but she didn't seem too surprised to see me, either. In the wind we strolled along the flat beach. Margit pointed at the sand dunes she was trying to help secure by planting out grass. She explained what she had been taught about the job, and talked about her new friends on the work team. I couldn't get her to say more about why she had changed her mind about us spending the summer together in Munich. We walked on in silence in the growing dusk. In the distance I made out the causeway, a line on the horizon barely visible between sea and sky. Then there was a plume of smoke, black against the afterglow, and a row of lights.

"That's the last train back to the mainland," Margit said. "Where are you sleeping tonight?"

Later I found a room that was empty except for a metal bed frame upended in one corner. My rucksack became my pillow. There was no glass in the window, but the weather was warm and close. The next morning I looked for Margit, but she was already gone out to work. I walked into the centre of Westerdorf and ate breakfast and watched the visitors strolling to the beach. Everybody seemed to be with someone else or part of a family. I wandered aimlessly around the town, waiting for evening so I could see Margit again.

Throughout the afternoon clouds piled up over the North Sea, towering like the mountains I knew at home, and glowing in the sun. This flat and exposed place wasn't for me. I wanted the buildings of the city around me, its streets and squares, its churches and palaces, its beautifully maintained gardens. I wanted to see the distant mountains bounding my world, and not the infinities of the tall sky that rose out of the haze where it met the enveloping sea.

That night Margit took pity on me and invited me to share the meal that her work team were going to prepare on the beach. I helped to build the fire and gave a couple of marks towards buying beer and wine. But Margit always ensured that there was at least one other person between us as we sat cross-legged on the sand.

The team supervisor passed me a mug of beer as he sat down heavily next to me. I discovered that he was a local man. And as the flames flickered on our circle of faces I found myself starting to confide in him.

"Our work teams always have a few members like your friend," he said gently. "They want to get away, have a total change of scene. There are many reasons for that. The Island is quite some change of scene. Perhaps she had some concern she wanted to get into perspective. Perhaps there was another person. That is always possible, yes?"

I nodded glumly.

"I could offer you a job with the team, but I do not think that would be a good idea. Your friend chose to come to Westenstrand. You did not, not really."

I finished my beer and got up. I felt dizzy for a moment and swayed slightly. The supervisor jumped up and steadied me. I thanked him.

"You know where you are going?" he asked.

"Yes. I do now."

There was a cold gust of wind off the sea.

The clouds were still building up in the west as I set out. The moon shone on the towering and billowing masses, reminding me more than ever of the mountains near my home. Further out the sea was ink. The lines of breakers, sweeping in and crashing up onto the beach at a faster and faster rate, glowed in the moonlight. I collected my rucksack and headed through the quiet town towards the railway station.

I knew that the last train of the day had departed, and as I walked I thought at first about waiting at the station to catch the first one in the morning. The street darkened as the moon was obscured by cloud. In the west the coming storm was swelling up and now covered a third of the sky. Lightning flashed and I heard the first low rumbles of thunder. I wanted to get off the island as fast as I could. At the railway station I followed a street leading off to one side. Soon there was a rusted metal fence through which I could see the tracks glinting in the intermittent moonlight. Before long there was a gap; I threw my rucksack over and squeezed through after it. Then I started to walk along the causeway to the mainland.

I reckoned on the journey taking me about two hours. So I hoped that I would be able to outrun the storm and find shelter on the mainland. As I walked, the causeway ahead seemed to become a sort of tunnel through the open air: constricted, straight and narrow, and yet exposed to wind, moon, and stars. Soon all there was were the railway tracks stretched out behind and in front of me. For all I could tell they were endless, and moving while I stood still. I kept a sense of direction by looking behind me at the scattered lights of Westerdorf and the clouds—now grown even more to a mighty semicircle like half an arena, stretching from north through west to south. The moon was hidden. The sea grew rougher. Even though I was treading carefully along the very centre of the causeway, on the highest part between the two tracks, I felt the spray on my face as the sea was whipped up by blasts of wind growing stronger. My clothes and hair grew damp. I hoped that the causeway had been built high enough not to get flooded by even the highest tide.

The minutes passed as I strode on, metre after metre piling up into kilometre after kilometre. Ahead of me the lights of the mainland slowly grew more distinct as they grew closer. Now there were flashes of lightning all over the sky every few seconds; the thunder was becoming an almost continuous low roar. Occasionally I stumbled in the darkness, but the ground was firm and usually smooth underfoot. I maintained my pace. I saw the beach stretching away on either side of me. The line of the tracks remained ahead of me, curving away into the night. A flash of lightning that seemed to last for about ten seconds lit up a rusting metal fence rising out of the surf. Firm land reappeared and I climbed over the fence and slipped down the embankment. My jacket got torn on sharp stones and rough grass, but I rolled onto the sand and lay there gazing up into the churning, roiling clouds sliding overhead. A large drop of freezing rain landed on my face. I picked myself up and ran, barely making it to the shelter of a railway workers' hut when the storm finally broke and my world became roaring wind, pounding waves, and rain heavier than any I could remember.

I woke up when someone shook my shoulder. Two men in the uniform of the State Railway looked down at me. Through the open door all was serene: the sky was a sharp blue and the beach was bathed in strong, hot sunshine. I told the workers that I was on a walking holiday and had taken shelter when the storm had caught me by surprise. They made coffee and gave me some bread. Sitting out in front of the hut I quickly became dry and warm. I said something about the best way to get to the path leading to the road.

"Not wanting a trip out to Westenstrand, then?"

I shook my head. "No. Maybe another time. That was some storm last night, wasn't it?"

The men laughed. "We've got to walk out there. It's been reported that the Ebertdamm was overwhelmed and there's at least one break in it. If that's right, the Island's on its own again for a while. God be thanked, there was no train out on the causeway."

"I come from the Island," the other worker said. "It'll be no hardship for us. We've all got boats. The ferries will get a lot of welcome business." He took a final gulp of his coffee, and emptied the dregs from his mug out onto the ground. "It was a tremendous storm. I only hope that there hasn't been too much damaged or shifted about. The surveyors and mapmakers will be well occupied."

The first worker laughed. "Everyone benefits, I think!"

I thanked them for the coffee and bread and got to my feet. The sun was warm on my face.

"So where are you going now, then, young man?" the Islander asked, as we shook hands all around.

I hesitated. I'd forgotten the name of the town close by where the railway station was. I couldn't walk along the shining railway tracks again. Then I knew for sure where I was heading to.

"Munich," I said.

I never saw Margit again. I expect we both understood that the map had changed. The past was buried like a coastal village inundated by shifting sands. Everything had been altered. The landscape of the future was new. And while as yet there were no accurate maps, but only tentative explorations, these would develop and grow in accuracy. Shape and form would grow into definition and, with effort, routes work themselves out.

Silver on Green

The month of May was Eduard Miklos's favourite, in his place of exile. Each year, as spring advanced into early summer, for a few short weeks the quiet, respectable, and secluded suburb of London where he had made his home—his refuge—was transformed. To Miklos, as Turnham Park drowsed in the May sunshine and unseasonable warmth, the suburb became a dream, a glowing painting by Raoul Dufy, almost the nearest thing that he had ever expected to think of as an earthly paradise.

Soon after his arrival in Turnham Park, Miklos had gravitated towards the small circle of internationally-minded artists, retired academics, younger shop-keepers and owners of small businesses who considered themselves the local cosmopolitan and bohemian set. Most were anti-protectionist and fervent supporters of the League of Nations. They had welcomed Miklos into their midst as an exotic addition to their number, and genuinely appreciated his sometimes acerbic (but always well intentioned) contributions to their debates in the Park Tavern or in the West View Tea Shop on The Green. Miklos shared his thoughts within this small circle of trusted friends and associates during a largely liquid lunch on one particularly spectacular day in late spring, in his second spring in Turnham Park. And as always they listened with interest.

"Early this morning I had to fulfil an appointment with a friend who works at the embassy of my country. He helps me to maintain connections, informing me of current and prospective political developments—or rather, the lack of them—in the present regime. Of course I do not need to explain that we met in a safe place—somewhere else than the embassy. I still have to be careful; and my, shall I say, informer, cannot allow himself to be seen keeping company with me in public. Afterwards I was in a dejected state of mind as I travelled back on the Tube. And then it seemed that everything conspired to make my stroll home from the station into a sensory experience of the highest order. As I looked up from the emerald of The Green, I saw, as if for the first time, over and above all, the sky: so blue and deep I felt that I would fall up into it if I had been able to jump high enough. And then the sun, almost white in its intensity, a diamond embedded in the cushion of the cloudless heavens. All growing plants seemed to have been transformed into riots of tumbling blossoms, white and pink clouds fallen to earth. The red brick of the houses blazed like beacons in the sunshine, their fire darkened by the contrast to the limitless sky. The somewhat darker red tiles of roofs floated above blossoming trees and the palely translucent green of those newly coming into leaf. Garden hedges were ramparts of fresh green growth; the white-painted fences and gates glistened with a painful intensity. Flowers were patches and blots of hot colour flicked across walls and grass. I encountered hardly anyone outside; once away from The Green and the shops there was almost no traffic. The only sounds were the songs of birds and the wind in the branches. In the shadows the air was still cool—as I breathed I could taste it, and it was sweet. I was downcast, but then I was raised up. Gentlemen, this morning I walked through the Garden of Eden."

For a moment the little group sat on in silence. Their corner of the lounge bar of the Park Tavern was quiet at the best of times, and the hot sunny air seemed to muffle all sounds apart from the slightest murmur of conversation and the clink of glasses. Then more ale was called for. Further cigarettes were lit and pipes refilled.

"So, my dear Miklos, this is the Garden of Eden—on the District Line?"

Miklos joined in with the laughter.

"Yes, are you sure you were ever a politician, Mr. Miklos?" said Richards, a young journalist who lived close by and who often joined the group on a nominally probational basis. "I don't expect poetry from our or anyone's leaders and representatives. High-flown rhetoric and colourful mendacity, to be sure, but not such an appreciation of what is, after all, only one of a number of types of ordinary morning that can occur at this time of year, and always in a thoroughly mundane place. Turnham Park is only London, after all, not Paradise!"

"Perhaps you are right," Miklos said after a pause. "Although when I had to leave my country and was able to settle here, Turnham Park did seem paradisiacal to me. It still does. I hope that I will never cease to be grateful for the chance to live here, to inhabit one of the small red houses set in a green garden bounded by a white fence. Of course, I do wish to return home, to the land of my birth, but until its Government can be cleansed and reformed . . . "

"And you attempt to play your part?" asked Richards. "You did say that you visited a countryman of yours—one who holds similar views to yours, I would assume?"

Miklos drained his glass. "I do not think that I care to discuss politics on such a day as this."

Shortly afterwards Richards left for his work in Fleet Street, and conversation moved on.

"Gentlemen, before I go on my way, I find I must mention politics, after all," Miklos said. "Our young friend asked if I had really been a politician. Yes, I realise the spirit in which he asked the question! Well, of course the answer really is yes. Resoundingly, I think you could say." Miklos gazed at the faces of his friends sitting at their table. "Yes, I have been a politician, and I think I will always be one, like my father and grandfather before me. I can't escape it. Now, earlier, I described Eden—although I intended no religious significance. But it will do; and I will continue the comparison, if that is the right word. And here is how one can tell that I once wielded power, and am at ease doing so. I ask you: If this is Eden, where is the serpent? Now you know my profession and calling for sure—because I must always be asking that question!"

As the laughter subsided, Miklos slowly took three large and heavy silver coins from the worn leather purse he always carried with him. He placed the coins in a pile on the table in front of his now vacant chair. And then, with a smile and a nod to his friends, he strolled out into the street.

In the tavern, Miklos had been careful to make sure that the coins he'd left behind were the florins that he'd intended to pay his share with. In his old purse he also carried a number of the silver coins of his own country: hefty and substantial pieces, similar to the British half crowns he cherished, but bearing the head of old King Stefan, the current King's father. He had quite a few more at home; almost enough, he thought, to count as a small hoard. Miklos made sure that all of the coins bore the heads of monarchs other than the young King Marius, who had ordered his expulsion from his native land.

As Miklos sat at the desk in his study, he found that he wasn't quite ready to begin writing the day's portion of his memoirs. He cleared away some unopened letters and newspapers and set out a row of coins in front of him. This time they were of the highest denomination that had been struck with the highest silver content. One of the things that Miklos's contact at the embassy had told him about was a forthcoming announcement from the National Bank that the amount of the precious metal in the national coinage was to be reduced. Miklos set out the coins like a grand master setting out his chess pieces, arranging them by date. They sparkled and glinted in the stray shafts of sunlight that reached through the windows and pierced the cool green dimness of the room. Miklos picked up a coin and set it on its edge, and started it spinning. For a few moments it became a whirling and insubstantial silver sphere before falling onto one of its faces and clattering across the desk. Then he took one of King George's new crown coins out of a drawer, flicking it into the air and catching it, repeating the action several times with ease, following the movements of the tumbling and glittering disk. Miklos knew he was wasting time amusing himself; it brought back happy memories from his childhood and ones that were not so good from more recent times. Miklos caught the coin in mid-air and examined it, looking at it closely as if he'd never seen it before. The design on the reverse had been controversial: the traditional rendering of Saint George and the Dragon had been changed to a stylised and obviously contemporary one. Richards had told him that the coin had been nicknamed the "rocking horse crown". Nevertheless Miklos had become used to the design with its sinuous dragon and now liked it. He replaced the shiny silver disk in the drawer, and took a fresh sheet of paper from the pile in a box under his desk.

Miklos felt that he had always served his monarch well. As a very young man he had joined his country's diplomatic service and served in several capacities at the embassy in London. Then he had returned home, and for many years sat in parliament, first as a member of the Chamber of Representatives and latterly of the Senate. From early in his career, Miklos had taken pains to make himself available. His wife had died shortly after their marriage; and, while not ceasing to mourn her and their stolen future, Miklos had henceforth courted no mistress but politics. And then it was with a heightened fervour. Old King Stefan had ensured that Miklos entered the Cabinet; he had held several portfolios, including that of Minister of the Interior. And he had twice served as Prime Minister. Miklos had never been under any illusion as to the nature of the regimes he served in or headed as the King's nominee. Whenever the King decided a change of government was needed, Miklos had accepted the result of the elections that followed and confirmed the King's decision. He had been convinced that the political party that his family had always supported, and its governments that he was associated with, always represented the highest number of people for the longest amount of time, and kept the nation stable and growing in prosperity. Miklos had wielded real power, and had enjoyed doing so—for the sake of the nation.

For the first year or so of his reign King Marius made no changes to the way the country was governed since the dynasty had been invited to rule over the newly independent nation. The last of the old King's governments had been dominated by the United Agrarians, with Miklos's Liberal Radical Party in opposition. But this hadn't worried him: the pendulum would swing back again sooner or later, and all pieces fall back into their accustomed places until the next time change was decreed. Miklos expected the Premiership to be his again. And then when he had indeed been appointed Prime Minister by the young and inexperienced King, he had assumed that the business of government would be carried on as before. That had been Miklos's only mistake.

Although it was still early afternoon, Miklos poured out a glass of the plum brandy specially imported from his native province. He started to think about the mistake that had cost him his political career. A few months into his second term of office, Miklos had been summoned to the Palace. There was nothing at all unusual in that. It was true that the adverse economic conditions prevailing throughout the world were making themselves felt at home; but the Miklos Government had measures in place, with more to be enacted. Some discontent was to be expected, but Miklos was sure that the King would be content to let his present Government tackle any dissent by the usual range of means, just as governments had always done.

The announcements and decrees had been prepared in advance. King Marius had informed his Prime Minister that all political parties were to be abolished, and the constitution revised to give the King a greater and more defined role in the political life of the nation. Henceforth there would be only one party allowed, and only that party would provide the members of the legislature not appointed by the King. All members of the Cabinet must be members of the party and be appointed by the Prime Minister, who would be appointed by the King. The King's appointee would lead the new party and the Government. Miklos would be required to organise a nationwide plebiscite to consult the people about the changes and ensure that they returned the correct result.

"Your Majesty, these 'reforms', as you call them, will result in nothing less than a dictatorship."

"That is correct, Mr. Miklos. Nevertheless I shall, of course, still require a Prime Minister. I expect to name you to that post."

"I would be reduced to being merely your puppet, Majesty. That is not how the position of Prime Minister was envisaged by our forefathers when we became independent seventy years ago. They were determined to avoid the domination of any one branch of the Executive—"

The King smiled. "I believe your grandfather's brother wrote our present, and I feel now sadly outworn, constitution, did he not?"

"Yes, Your Majesty."

"Mr. Miklos, you may be the named author of the new one, if you wish. But I have to tell you now that this nation needs my Royal Dictatorship, and it will get it. Whether or not you agree or are a part of it. You may choose. And now."

"Your Majesty, I resign."

"Very well. Good evening."

The King held out his hand, but Miklos bowed stiffly and stalked out of the room.

The decrees were splashed across the front pages of the following morning's newspapers. Miklos awoke to find armed gendarmes placed at all entrances and exits to his house, and at the gates and outside the high walls around the garden.

Miklos had covered several large sheets of paper with his minute and angular handwriting before he stopped. While resting, he read over what he had written, whispering certain phrases and sentences back to himself. "House arrest. For my own protection and safety, they said." Miklos snorted in disgust, and realised that his fists were clenched in anger and feelings of betrayal, just as they had been when he'd left the Palace on the night of his resignation.

To begin with, Miklos's study and library had been placed out of bounds to him. Doors and windows had been locked and guarded. The telephone had been disconnected. Apart from those violations of his property and possessions—he knew the law that gave the authorities the right, having drafted it himself—they had allowed him to have the run of his own house and garden. But once he had been denied access to his books and papers, Miklos would spend most of the day in bed, or sit at the vast table in the kitchen drinking coffee or plum brandy, or wander aimlessly around the garden. His servants had been dismissed; his meals were prepared somewhere outside and brought to him by one of the gendarmes. Items such as knives and scissors had vanished from the house; but the possibility of escape through injury or even suicide never entered Miklos's mind.

One morning Miklos was strolling in the garden when he heard laughter. He turned and walked towards the sound. At one of the strong wrought-iron gates— now locked—that pierced the wall, Miklos found the two young gendarmes stationed there apparently waving their arms in the air as they continued to laugh. Their merriment ceased the moment they saw Miklos approaching; they immediately stood to attention, trying not to look guilty. Miklos noticed that both men had their hands clenched into fists. He smiled and nodded at the officers, and strolled on past them. A few moments later, when he thought they would have relaxed again, he suddenly stopped and turned.

"Can we help you, sir?" one of the gendarmes asked.

"What have you got in your hands, both of you?"

The young men looked at each other. It was clear that they had never expected the former Prime Minister to speak to them, let alone ask such a question.

"Come on, show me."

Both officers held out their hands like naughty children and unclenched their fists. A large silver coin nestled in each palm.

"And what were you doing with your money?"

"Juggling, sir."

"I beg your pardon?"

The other gendarme spoke up. "We was juggling, sir. You know, like this." Without any self-consciousness the man started to juggle the two coins he had been holding. Miklos saw the swift glint of silver in the sun, moving smoothly from hand to hand. He was mesmerised. "Come on," the gendarme said. Two more glints joined the first two: his companion had flung his coins expertly into the game. The gendarmes started to laugh again, as the juggling continued effortlessly.

"Remarkable," Miklos muttered to himself. Despite himself, he started to smile. Then he told the policeman to stop.

"We're sorry, sir," the man said. "It won't happen again, I promise. You won't say anything, will you, sir? Please?"

"Don't worry," he said. "I won't say anything, for now at least. But I think both of you had better get back to work."

Back in the house Miklos went through the pockets of all his suits and checked the contents of a strongbox he kept at the bottom of a cupboard in his dressing room.

He soon assembled some forty silver coins, which he placed in rows on the kitchen table. He arranged them by denomination and date; he turned over any coins bearing King Marius's head, so he didn't have to look at it. Then Miklos picked up two of the coins, and felt their weight, balancing one on each palm.

Several hours later Miklos had trained himself to juggle two coins with reasonable accuracy. He no longer sent the coins flying around the room every few seconds, rolling across the floor under chairs and into every nook and cranny. For the first time since his arrest Miklos went to bed in a good mood, and looked forward to getting up the next morning.

After another week, the doors of his study and library were unlocked and Miklos was allowed to use them once more. The rooms had been searched thoroughly; he soon discovered that certain private and political papers had been removed. But apart from the missing items, there was little in the way of damage and disruption. He was also allowed to receive a few carefully screened visitors. But Miklos neglected his books and papers, and spent as much time as he could in the kitchen. Making sure he was never observed—as best he could— Miklos continued to train himself to juggle silver coins, improving his dexterity and skill. He gradually traded and exchanged the new coins of King Marius in his possession for older examples bearing the likenesses of the royal predecessors.

Every morning Miklos arranged his coins on the kitchen table, positioned in their ranks like an army about to begin manoeuvres or as if some sort of game were about to be started. When he wasn't trying to juggle them, Miklos examined his coins minutely, weighing them in his hands one against the other, or in measured combinations. His eyes were continually drawn to the polished glint of new silver and the steady dull sheen of the more circulated and worn coins. He developed a fascination for the simple fact of *silver* in its coined form. Miklos held to its solidity and mass. For once he had something to grasp—and often literally. The congealed moonlight of silver pooled in his hand represented firm value, a bulwark against uncertainty. He explored his coins, fingering them with his eyes closed and holding them to his nose to smell. He tasted the metal. Shape and form spoke to him. And silver entered Miklos's soul.

A visitor was announced while Miklos was sitting in a rocking chair on the terrace outside his study. One of the two gendarmes accompanying the visitor placed a chair close to where Miklos sat, and then stood back, with his colleague, at a respectful distance.

"Senator Artur Ozera, sir."

Miklos stood and embraced the Secretary-General of the now banned Liberal Radical Party, who was also Miklos's brother-in-law. Then Miklos invited him to sit down.

"Artur, so much has changed! Tell me, do you find *me* changed? Because I am. I might not look it, but I am."

"I had better come straight to the point, Eduard. I have a message from His Majesty—unofficially, you understand, but he means it. The King wants you to reconsider your resignation. He would like to dismiss that lapdog Troester and appoint you Prime Minister instead.

Not immediately, of course; you would rejoin the Cabinet first. His Majesty is prepared to let it be known that your resignation and, ah, sojourn here were due to an illness. The King would say that you have made a full recovery and he is pleased to welcome you back as the head of his Royal Government. What can I tell the King?"

"Marius wants me for another of his lapdogs, is that it? All right, I understand that. But tell me, Artur, what if I decline to fall in with the young King's wishes?"

"Eduard, you will be expelled from the country," Ozera said. "Exile is the only alternative to accepting the King's offer."

"So be it. Exile it is. Will you stay to dinner, Artur? I am sure they can bring in some extra food and wine, if I have a guest."

Ozera shook his head. "I am sorry, Eduard. I had better go straight on to the Palace. I can't say I'm surprised at your answer. And I must say I'm glad. You have not let the party down, Eduard, even now."

They shook hands, and began to walk towards the garden gate. The two gendarmes followed.

"How long will I have?" Miklos asked.

"Not long. A few days, I think. I do believe the King will be expecting the answer that I'll be giving, so he will act quickly. But I don't think he will be ungenerous. He isn't a complete fool."

"And you, Artur? Are you remaining with this King?"

Ozera shrugged his shoulders. "Who knows? Perhaps I will be joining you, somewhere, sooner or later."

As soon as Ozera had left, Miklos started making firm plans. When the news of his going into exile was announced a week later, Miklos was ready.

❧

Turnham Park had not been as unknown to Miklos as it still was to most of the inhabitants of the teeming city surrounding it. During his first time in London—when he had been employed at his country's embassy—Miklos had lived in the quiet suburb. He had wanted to live in a place away from the noisy and dusty West End, but which was yet easily accessible from it. Turnham Park had fulfilled his expectations and needs. In the cool evenings Miklos enjoyed strolling around The Green, with its dewy grass and ancient trees and mixture of old and new houses. And the new red-brick church, tavern, Community Institute, and parade of shops had catered to most of his other needs, whether actual or potential. The suburb was out of the way, yet hidden in plain sight close to the crowded main road leading out of the conurbation to the west. Turnham Park was little known and seldom visited; a "blank" on the street-map, a terra incognita that it was easy to miss or ignore.

When Miklos lived in the suburb for the first time, it had still been just on the farthest western edge of the city. A few fields, market gardens, and old houses survived, although in most places the city's edge had overflowed and swallowed them, the twisting lanes being transformed into raw streets of identical black and white villas. After the Great War—from which Miklos's country had emerged transformed by huge additions to its territory—the new orbital road was constructed not so very far to the west of Turnham Park; but the suburb had become quite insulated by then. It continued to dream away the years on its own terms, sunlit and tranquil even as the constant traffic rumbled to and fro along the main road and the electric trains arrived sind departed from the station by The Green. But at night roofs and trees were silhouetted against the constant livid glow in the sky, and all but the brightest stars were dimmed by the vast pool of light that was London.

Miklos's plans had proceeded smoothly. By the time he arrived in London, the house in Turnham Park had been bought and prepared for him. As Ozera had predicted, King Marius had not chosen to be vindictive, and no obstacles had been placed in Miklos's way. He had been allowed to take his books and papers with him into exile, while his bank accounts and investments had been left untouched. An official from the embassy had been deputed to meet Miklos upon his arrival in London, and to ensure that he was introduced to the appropriate authorities, before escorting him to his hotel. Miklos was not unknown in England; during his years in politics his name had often attracted as much notoriety as bemused approval. And now the circumstances of his departure from his native land were of considerable interest to many. Miklos gave interviews to the leading newspapers, answered questions, and allowed photographs to be taken. When he was left alone at last in his suite, he unwrapped the small parcel that had been left for him, taking out the key and turning it over, wiping it with his handkerchief before attaching it to the chain he always carried with him. The next afternoon Miklos opened the front door of his house in Turnham Park as if he had lived there for many years and had merely returned home after a short holiday or from work early.

The life of Turnham Park's little bohemian set orbited, in an intricate dance, around three places of illumination and nourishment. There were the Park Tavern, the West View Tea Shop, and the Community Institute. The Community

Institute was a bulky red-brick structure built in a free and relaxed gothic style. There was an echoing timber-roofed hall with numerous meeting and other rooms attached to it. Standing behind an immaculate stretch of lawn and flowerbeds, and shaded by several old elms, the Community Institute had a distinctly ecclesiastical appearance, although any connection with any church or other religious organisation was forbidden by the Institute's rules, which were rigorously enforced. In any case, the Rector of St. Jude's Church and the Minister of the Turnham Park Free Congregation were both active members of the Management Committee.

Although Miklos did not attend services at either church, he was well-known to their members and clergy, and so to the Institute's Management Committee. It was Richards who had finally talked him into it. The Committee had arranged a series of talks on the "Current and Future European Situation" and wanted Miklos to contribute. At first he had expressed doubts—not about his ability or the value of what he would say—but as to how advisable his taking part would be. He told Richards that he was a guest in the country. He didn't want to take the risk of saying anything—even inadvertently— that could offend the Royal Dictatorship at home, and give it cause to make difficulties for him with the British Government. But when the news came that Artur Ozera had been assassinated in the street outside his house, and, despite official denials, there was clear evidence that the King and his senior ministers knew about it, Miklos changed his mind and agreed to speak at the last of the series of talks.

Except for the talk given by H.G. Wells, Miklos's contribution to the series was by far the best attended. It wasn't every day that a hall in a London suburb could boast an ex-Prime Minister. Miklos's feelings of outrage and disgust over the death of the man who had been not only his trusted political friend and colleague, but also one of his closest relatives, hadn't left him, and he left the audience filling the hall in no doubt about that. But towards the end of his allotted time Miklos departed from his carefully prepared text. "In my country the Government is now in the hands of the palace camarilla that surrounds the King like a poisonous miasma. And the King himself is the main source of the infection, and approves and encourages it. He and they are unaccountable and, for the present at least, unassailable. Ladies and Gentlemen: I, and many of us, live here in this sunny and safe suburb; and I had come to think that I may very well have to live out the rest of my days in it. Now it seems that there is no prospect of returning to the country I love above all others—and I have to say that even in the light of my tremendous gratitude to the British Government and the people of Great Britain for welcoming me here and allowing me to live among you. Perhaps my life will be taken from me now, by, as it were, the long arm of the camarilla reaching out and beating me down. So be it. I want to live, and I celebrate life, here; but I can say to you that I also have no terrors in dying for my country, at whichever time and by whatever agency."

Miklos had given Richards a copy of his text as a favour, but even as he spoke, the journalist had jotted down Miklos's closing words in shorthand. The account published in his newspaper thus contained what Miklos had actually said to his audience. When he read Richards's account and the quotations he had used, Miklos realised that he might be more of a prophet than he thought possible. Even so, he began to take precautions. Before going to bed he checked and double-checked that all doors and windows were locked and secure. He started to take extra care when he left his house, looking around him for signs of any unusual activity that might have taken place. When he was out and about he tried to observe the faces of the people he passed in the street, and to remember them. He kept his distance from anyone he didn't know. But above all, Miklos did everything he could to ensure that meetings with his circle of friends were not disrupted, or any of them exposed to danger.

First of all Miklos took Richards into his confidence. Then, one damp and misty evening when the little group sat in their accustomed places in the Park Tavern, he told them plainly what he thought the possibilities could be, and the consequences. There was quiet but sincere indignation. Miklos's friends were troubled that one of their number could feel himself to be in such danger. There was talk about asking for police protection or employing a bodyguard. But Miklos thanked them for their concern and reassured them, asking only that they tell him if anyone were to make enquiries about him, his daily routines or whereabouts. "One more thing, gentlemen," Miklos said. "I do also have this." He pulled a small pistol out from inside his jacket. "And I can assure you that my possession of this weapon is fully legal!"

Miklos was the last to leave. He drained his glass and stood up to reach for his overcoat and hat where they hung on a convenient hook. Coins jingled in his pocket as he moved. Miklos found two half crowns and a silver coin of King Stefan. For a moment he stood still, smiling; then, in the fading firelight of the bar, as nobody was looking, he began to juggle with the three coins. For a few moments his movements were sure, and the coins flew, circling from hand to hand. Then Miklos was distracted by a slight cough from the shadows, and the spell was broken. The two half crowns ended up in the same hand, while the other coin hit the edge of the table and fell onto the floor, rolling away into the gloom. Miklos was unwilling to lose the coin, and immediately knelt down and began to search for it, feeling around under the table. He saw the glint of silver, and reached for it. As he stood up again, he weighed the coin in his palm. Something was wrong. He held up the coin to examine it better in the dying light of the fire, and saw the sharp and as yet unworn profile of King Marius.

"This one's yours," the voice said. "Here." A tall man loomed out of the near darkness, and held out Miklos's coin. "And you can keep that new one, Mr. Miklos."

"Who are you?" Miklos whispered. "The serpent?"

They sat in Miklos's study, sipping plum brandy. The stranger had brought a bottle of an exclusive and expensive brand with him from the capital.

"I think I heard you say 'serpent' earlier on," he said. "What did you mean? Mr. Miklos, this place is not Eden, surely? I would've thought that the mountains and high woods and steep valleys of your home province would be your Eden."

Miklos did not reply. His visitor paused before speaking again.

"You need not be banned from it. Artur Ozera sent me. I regret that I have only just been able to carry out his commission and come to you." Again he paused.

"Please tell me who you really are before you continue," Miklos said softly. "I will do you the courtesy of hearing you out, whoever you are and whatever you want." Miklos plucked the new silver coin from his pocket and placed it on the table between him and his guest. He turned the coin over, hiding King Marius's head. The coat of arms of his country glinted in the lamplight.

"My name is not important. If your contacts are still loyal, you can find out easily enough. But there's really no need for you to bother. As I said, Artur Ozera sent me. The King wishes you to return. His Majesty will reinstate you. You know that General Pitu is gaining influence in the country and over the King. You must know that unless he can name you as Prime Minister, the time will shortly come when he must name General Pitu. You are the only man with the authority to stand up to the General. Either you return as Prime Minister or Pitu will take over the Government. He might even overthrow the King and rule through Prince Andreas."

"Andreas is not yet fifteen!"

"Precisely. There will need to be a Council of Regency. Pitu will be Chairman and dominate it. The Prince will have to sign whatever Pitu tells him to. Pitu will rule—"

Miklos slammed his glass down on the table, slopping plum brandy onto the surface. "I said I would hear you out, but I cannot listen to this!" he shouted. He made a calming gesture with his right hand. "No, no, Mr. Anonymous, no-one can hear—we are alone. Now listen to me. Artur Ozera would never have done what you say. I know—knew—him too well. Ozera is the only man who could have done what you propose, if he hadn't been murdered. Tell me, did you shoot him? Was it you? And will you kill me too, if I do not give you the answer Marius wants to hear? Or will you commit another murder anyway? Or is it actually Pitu who sent you?"

The stranger sighed. "I will answer your questions. I speak for His Majesty the King. I make you a genuine offer from him. I was not the man who shot Artur

Ozera—but I could be the man to shoot you, yes. I will return at eight o'clock tomorrow night. I will expect your answer. You should not leave this house in the meantime. Depending on what your answer is, I will decide on what must be done. Both our lives are involved, Mr. Miklos. Good night."

Miklos's visitor had left the bottle of plum brandy on the table. Miklos smiled wryly as he poured himself another glass. He took out his worn leather purse and placed its contents on the table. Then he opened a drawer in his desk and removed a small velvet bag. A shiny metallic stream poured out onto the table next to the silver already there. Miklos picked out five coins and started to juggle them, as if in a trance. He continued without a break or error for several minutes. Then he stopped and laid out all the coins on the table, shuffling them around until he created the right shape. He put the new coin in the middle of the pattern. He groaned as he saw that King Marius's profile was facing upwards, but he left the coin as it was and turned the others face down. Finally Miklos gathered together all the British silver coins he could find, and surrounded the others with a ring of florins and half crowns. He drank another glass of plum brandy. For a moment he wondered if the bottle was left behind because something had been added to it while he wasn't looking.

The study grew dim as the fire faded. Miklos got up to switch on more lamps, but decided to light candles instead. The fire and candlelight lent the tarnished silver candlesticks a dull radiance while the coins laid out on the table glittered and glinted in the flickering flames. Miklos sat back, gazing at the silver coins spread out in front of him. Eventually the great shape he had made started to absorb all his sight and attention. To him the shapes and forms on the coins flowed and merged. Miklos heard the voices of King Stefan and King Marius; he recalled the encouraging words that King Stefan's father, Mihail II, had graciously addressed to him in his quavering voice when he had been a child. The silver shapes waxed and waned like phases of the moon, but the form endured and deep within silver remained constant. The very invocation of the pale metal, proving worthy of trust and true to form, entered into the stamped and shaped shields and devices—and passive was transformed into active. Warm air shimmered and the shadows grew darker. And in the room Miklos closed his eyes and did not move.

It was Richards's newspaper that broke the story first. Overnight, events had moved swiftly. A coup had taken place in the capital city of Miklos's country. King Marius's Royal Dictatorship had been overthrown by General Pitu, who had declared himself Leader and sent the King into exile. Marius had been flown out of the country just before dawn. Pitu confirmed his own and his new Government's unconditional loyalty to King Andreas.

As the sun rose over Fleet Street, Richards hastened westwards to see Miklos. Further details of the coup had been received over the wires. "I knew Salazar would take Marius in," the journalist said to himself as his taxi sped towards Hammersmith. But no announcement had yet been made about Eduard Miklos and his possible return from exile. Richards dismissed the taxi and walked up to the front door of Miklos's house. The paved footpath was damp and in shadow; the lawn was covered in dew. Red roofs and walls glowed in the rising sun. Richards rang the bell and waited. After a few minutes he walked around the side of the house to where the French windows of Miklos's study opened onto a small patio. The metal handle was cold and covered in dew, but Richards pushed it down, and the door opened.

"Hello? Mr. Miklos? Are you there? It's me, Richards."

There was no reply. The house seemed to be empty. Richards found no sign of Miklos, and no sign that he had gone out or been forced to leave. When the police came, the inspector in charge asked about the blank silver disks scattered across the table next to the empty bottle of plum brandy and expired candles. Richards said that he couldn't explain them. But before the police arrived he had noticed one other object on the table, which he had gently wrapped in a piece of dark green velvet before slipping it into his coat pocket. Now he felt it pulling the fabric down—the burden of the tiny silver figure of Eduard Miklos. It was utterly lifelike, perfectly reproducing every detail of Miklos's clothing and appearance. Richards thought it was strange that Miklos had never mentioned the statuette or shown it to him.

Later Richards returned to the newspaper office to start work on his story. Even as he wrote, more news from Miklos's country began to come through. He thought about the politician. As the day wore on, the situation continued to develop, and the journalist found he had a great many more things to think about.

Winter's Traces

Notes on William Winter

William Winter, a prolific composer of light orchestral music, died recently at the age of eighty-eight. He was born in London. The only child of a railway ticket clerk, Winter retained an interest in railways all his life, explaining that some of the rhythmic and atmospheric effects in many of his compositions were inspired by trains. Winter was an honorary member of several railway trade unions and was a generous contributor to railway employees' charities and benevolent associations. After leaving school at the age of fifteen, Winter followed in his father's footsteps and went to work in the ticket office at Euston Station. He was a largely self-taught musician, working as a cinema organist in his spare time. Winter soon found himself in demand due to the high technical quality of his playing and the inventiveness of his improvisations, and gave up his job at Euston. Winter was "discovered" by Eric Coates when he wrote to the composer to suggest some changes in a piece he had heard at a concert. Coates recognised Winter's talent and helped him to gain commissions for numerous orchestral concert pieces for radio and short information films. Winter's most successful and well-known work was undoubtedly *Lines Under London*. Characteristically nicknamed "Music Down the Tube" by the composer himself, it was a reworking of short film pieces originally commissioned by London Transport for films about the London Underground. The opening fanfare of the movement "Northern and Central" achieved particular fame when London Transport experimented with broadcasting music in its trains and stations. However, the trial was not a success and was quickly discontinued. Winter was a comparative latecomer to the field of orchestral light music, which during the 1960s largely vanished from the airwaves and the repertoire. Winter's subsequent endeavours to develop the variety and scope of his work were not successful, and his "serious" or "classical" music received little, if any, recognition. In his later years Winter became a virtual recluse, maintaining only a minimal contact with the outside world by letter, and later, email. William Winter died in London. He was—

In exasperation I saved the file and sat back in my chair. Writing "just a few words" about William Winter was proving to be more difficult than I'd expected. There was so little to go on. Most of what I had found came from a rarely-visited website designed and maintained by an enthusiast of light orchestral music who had somehow tracked down Winter in 2006 and persuaded him to give a short interview by email. Apparently Winter had embraced computing and the internet; although the interview hadn't said so, it had clearly provided Winter with a way to maintain his seclusion while keeping in contact with events and a very small and select number of people.

I have no special interest in Winter's music, or that of composers like him. And I am certainly not interested in railways, whether above or below the ground. But I value the understated technical mastery of the form that the light music composers clearly possessed. The evocative qualities of their music are a constant delight. A snatch of melody can transport me to a lost world that I'm not old enough to have ever possessed: the world of cinema newsreels, half crowns, hats, the Empire, glowing valves of warming-up radio sets and the smell of scorching dust, mantelpieces, steam locomotives, art deco, the novels of Nevil Shute, and much, much else from a decent and quiet era that never really existed. The music sustains and nourishes the illusion. And as for railways, in the illusory world the trains always ran on time; but in reality I use them as little as possible, preferring the certainties gained by being able to drive to my destination.

Picking up the phone I spoke to the owner of the light music website. Perhaps I hinted that I was considering a full-length biography of William Winter, or at least knew a publisher who would be interested. In any case by the time I rang off he'd promised to ask Winter's companion if there were any objections to me visiting the house and asking some questions. My contact hadn't mentioned anything about a widow, so I assumed that Winter's companion was a nurse or care worker, or even a housekeeper. I realised that I hadn't asked what her name was. I closed the Winter file and put in some more work on another project. William Winter could wait a day or two. If nothing came of contacting the nurse, I could probably get away with sending in the piece more or less as I'd already written it, with perhaps the addition of a few quotes from record sleeves and another mention of Winter's reclusive tendencies. By the time I switched off my laptop I'd parked Winter and his music on a shelf at the back of my mind, out of the way but where I could find it again without too much effort.

When I first go to my email each morning I always open the junk folder and quickly scroll through the spam waiting in it. Just because I don't know the sender doesn't always mean that I don't want to receive the message. The following day was no exception. There was the usual crop of emails from the daughters of recently deceased African generals who needed my help in releasing the millions of dollars that had been lovingly put aside for them. There were a large number of emails from ladies beseeching me for a photo and offering one of theirs. I was just about to delete the lot when I noticed a message with "William Winter" as the subject heading. I moved the email to my inbox and opened it.

As I'd hoped, the email was from Winter's companion. It was signed Chris, and invited me to visit her at Winter's house in order to discuss the possibilities of writing about him. There was no mention of what sort of writing was expected, or how much, but there were hints that there were plenty of potential research materials available. I thought it a little odd that Winter's nurse or housekeeper seemed to be in a position to grant (or presumably deny) access to them. Chris didn't explain why the owner of the light music website hadn't already been allowed the opportunity to get at Winter's papers—unless he had been, and the result had not proved pleasing. I hoped that I was being given the chance because it was known that I was a professional with a proven journalistic and literary track record. In any case, the implication was that I could be in on the ground floor with any posthumous William Winter industry. I replied straight away. Before long I'd arranged with Chris for me to visit and conduct a preliminary interview. I had left my options open, hinting that the end result could be anything from the short obituary or appreciation that I'd already been commissioned to write, up to a multi-volume illustrated biography. I sent a final email of thanks and attached the draft of my notes.

William Winter had lived in inner Metroland—deep in the tangle of tree-lined streets, small parks, and industrial estates filling the wedge of north-west London between Western Avenue and the Edgware Road, and extending out a mile or so beyond the North Circular Road. As far as I could determine, his house was located in one of the outer and better parts of Neasden, although it might possibly have counted as Dollis Hill. Looming out of the distance I saw the new Wembley Stadium aground on a serried mass of rooftops; its colossal metal arch dominated the skyline. There was a large and steeply rising park with long, gently curving roads following the terraced contours. Every street corner seemed to have its own small shopping parade with grimy art deco trimmings. Winter's house was also embedded in the knotted skeins of Tube and railway lines, junctions, sidings, goods yards and train depots that spread across the area. I parked the car in the short cul-de-sac that I'd eventually hunted down on the map. As I stood in the sunlit quiet, I knew that I had entered the very epitome of English Home Counties suburbia. I hadn't realised that such places still existed, and certainly not so close in to the centre of the London sprawl. There was a constant muted background roar from the traffic on the North Circular, and I could hear the distant clattering of Tube trains. But the birdsong was louder. In the street most of the garden gates were still the original wooden ones, beautifully looked after, clean and shining with bright paint. The gables of the semi-detached houses still had the rising sun designs to match the garden gates: no fake wood cladding here. White pebble-dashed walls glowed in the sun behind well-maintained trees and clipped hedges. Most of the windows I could see retained the small panels of stained glass in their upper sections. There were no plastic doors and window frames, no satellite dishes visible. For a moment I wondered if I'd slipped back in time. I expected that the first thing I'd notice in Winter's house would be the three ducks silently and eternally flying in formation across the wall.

The gate swung open on well-oiled hinges and clicked shut behind me. There was an old-fashioned manual lawnmower next to the path by the step up to the porch; the front door was lost in shadow. Thinking of the mower as old-fashioned seemed an impertinence. I was out of place, not the machine. It looked almost as good as new, although it could easily have been bought half a century ago. I was about to raise the door knocker when I heard a cheery voice behind me.

"Good morning! Good morning!"

I turned to see a short, broad-shouldered, vigorous man beaming at me. He wore black trousers and an open-necked white shirt which glowed brilliantly in the sunshine. The sleeves were rolled up to above his elbows, revealing muscular and tanned arms. He had a full head of thick white hair brushed straight back. I guessed the man was about sixty or possibly a little older. He gestured at the mower.

"I always keep the grass cut short. Helps keeps me fit, you know. I'm going to see about looking after one or two other gardens round here now I've got time on my hands. Some of the old people aren't too with it these days. But I'm still going strong!"

The last thing I wanted to do was to get into a long conversation with the gardener, no matter how friendly and lively he was. "I've come to see, ah, Mr. Winter's— no, I mean, Mrs—no, sorry, I only know her name is Chris. The late Mr. Winter's, er, we arranged it by email." I reached out for the door knocker again.

The man nodded, still smiling. "Yes, that's right, with Chris. That's me. Christopher Strande. Come in."

In the front sitting room Strande invited me to sit down while he went and made tea. It looked as if I'd been right about the house. There was no flight of ducks, but apart from that it seemed to be a shrine to the years immediately preceding the Second World War. The stained glass in the upper part of the bay window spangled the art deco carpet with molten multicoloured shapes. The sofa and armchairs were deeply upholstered in a black and white fabric of triangles and circles, all jagged edges and sweeping curves. There was a tiled fireplace and mantelpiece. In the corner was a tall wooden radio cabinet shaped like the Cenotaph, and not much smaller. I imagined that I would hear Edward VIII's abdication speech if the radio were to be switched on.

Strande returned with tea and biscuits on a stainless steel tray. When he'd poured out the tea, Strande explained about the house. "The whole place is exactly like it would've been in the 1930s, when William was a child. He wanted it like that. I'll show you around. He did go in for the latest technology, though. Loved it, always did. Never let it control him, though. He always decided how to use it. So there's a new computer in William's study. We were going to convert some of his records, the 78s, into digital format, keep them on the computer."

I nodded politely. Strande had piercing eyes; I felt that I was being scanned and inspected. "When we've finished our tea, I'll show you William's personal archive. He had the garage made into a special room. All his music and recordings are in there."

A few minutes later we went out into the back garden and around the side of the house. Strande unlocked a door. "This was the garage," he said. He switched on the light. There was a desk and a battered sofa in the middle of the room. Against the far wall, where the garage door would have been, was a row of filing cabinets, with a large record player on top of them. Most of the walls were hidden by shelves crammed with folders of sheet music and rows of gramophone records. Framed posters advertising concerts or the release of a new piece of music covered most of the remaining wall space. There were no windows. "This is all William's music, his life," Strande said. "But it isn't everything he had. In the back bedroom upstairs he kept his collection of Eric Coates's music and recordings and memorabilia. Coates was always William's favourite. He always used to tell me that he owed his real start in music to Coates. All the stuff by other composers that William had is up there as well. There's tons of it."

"How many pieces did Mr. Winter write?" I asked. I knew my question must have sounded lame and banal.

"Hundreds," Strande replied. "Look around. All William's work is in chronological order."

There was row upon row of neatly bound manuscript books. Each bore a label stuck on its spine with the month and year written in. I touched one of the books. "May I have a look?"

Strande nodded.

I selected a book at random and pulled it out. It was for June 1975. When I opened it, I expected to see pages covered with musical notation—not immaculately written, but at least intelligible to anyone who could read music.

But instead I saw page after page of scribble, crossings-out, and doodling. Some pages had marks on them recognisable as music, but even then they were written over and scored through by thick ink lines. Many pages were blank except for a single line of notes that had been scribbled out. I replaced the book and looked through several more. They were all like the first one I'd opened. Some were almost entirely filled with expletives, single words and phrases, the same few repeated endlessly, scrawled and smeared over the pages. There were drawings, too. I'm not a prude, but I found a lot of those pages shocking, if only for the sheer amount of time and effort that had been devoted to them. And yet the books were the opposite of creation.

"Now you know," Strande said. "Almost everything William tried to write after about 1969 is like that. Meaningless. Utter rubbish."

"Why?"

Strande took the manuscript book out of my hands and carefully put it back in its place. "Let's sit down. Now then, you're not really very interested in William Winter's life and work, are you?" I started to protest, but Strande smiled and held up his hand. "It's all right. I understand. You've been given a job to do. You're a professional. You'll do what you're asked, to the best of your ability. William was the same, except he wrote music."

I nodded. "But in his last years? Hang on, no, not just in his last years. For about the last forty years of his life he couldn't compose, but filled books with stuff like that? Why? That was for nearly half his lifetime. What happened?"

"Do you really want to know?"

"Yes. I know I haven't been given a great deal of space, but if I can turn in a good piece, get people interested, there might be a further opportunity. Here's a composer who wasn't able to compose, and no-one knew, right? That could be of interest to many people, bring them to the music that was loved in his lifetime." I looked around the cramped room. "Perhaps if there's time I could hear something by Winter? His most popular piece, *Lines Under London*? Then you can tell me something about him, or I could come back. How long did you know him?"

"I've got plenty of time. I'll put on the record. If you haven't heard *Lines Under London* before, you're in for a very pleasant experience. There was talk about issuing it on CD, but it hasn't come to anything yet. Yes. We'll listen to this. Then I'll tell you a bit about William. And what happened, so you'll understand."

The music opened with a jaunty fanfare that seemed strangely familiar. By the time the piece ended I felt that I'd spent time listening to every memorable and classic English film tune and evocative musical theme that I'd ever heard; every archive radio programme and piece of background music used to evoke the varied moods of London during the years between the world wars. I shook my head. "I'm sure I've never heard that before," I said. "And yet it's always been a part of me."

We remained seated in the crowded room. Then Strande said, "I never liked it in here. It's too dark and stuffy. I never knew why William didn't keep his stuff upstairs, where it's fresh and light, and put everything else in here. But William would sometimes spend hours in here. Let's go back in the house. If we need anything from here we can come back."

Strande made more tea and brought in a large plate of sandwiches. "I made them myself, had them all ready. I did all the cooking," he said. "I did the garden and kept the house clean as well. I did it all for William. He wrote the music and set the mood. I kept everything going for him."

I ate a sandwich, then another, and waited for Strande to continue talking. My notebook was open on the little art deco table next to where I was sitting. Eventually I picked up my pen and broke the silence. "Earlier you said that Winter should've kept his archive upstairs, but he preferred to keep it in the converted garage. You seemed to imply that he wanted to hide his work away in the dark, instead of having it more easily available in the light. Is that right? Have I understood you correctly?"

Strande smiled. "Maybe that's right," he said. "There were times when William wanted to hide away in the dark. As you know, for about the last twenty years or so he very rarely went out. Even beyond the garden gate. William never wanted to see anyone. He said that all the composers he had any respect for, and who'd ever had any for him, were dead. He had no friends left except for me. It wasn't quite as bad as that. But sometimes I think it was as if he wanted to bury himself alive here."

"Why do you think that was? Had something happened to him? Was it connected to what you said about his music?"

"It was nearer fifty years ago that William turned his back on the world. So it forgot him and his music in exchange. But it was all connected. The real trouble came a bit later. When he'd had a bit too much to drink he told me he thought everything was because of me, but I don't think he believed that, not really. There was more than one reason. But they were all to do with him. It was William."

"Because of you? But you were his only friend. As well as his housekeeper, cook, and companion?"

Strande fixed me with a sudden glare. "Yes, I was all of those. He said *I* happened to him!"

My pen slipped. Then it dawned on me. "Oh I see. Well, I think I do."

"You've realised? Good. I don't know if anyone else ever did. It all just happened. I worked on the Tube, at the Neasden Depot. It's still there, a huge place. I lived in Harlesden at the time. I was still living at home with my parents. I cycled to and from work every day, whatever the weather. So I was flying down Dudden Hill Lane on my bike, and this bloke steps off the pavement and walks right into my path. I rang my bell and shouted, but he ignored me. Later I found out it was because he was trying out tunes in his head. Running them through his thoughts like trains through tunnels, as I remember he put it. I used the brakes, but I was going too fast to stop in time. I swerved just before I would've hit him and I went over the handlebars and ended up flat out on the road. Luckily I was finishing a night shift and there was hardly any traffic. William had been awake all night running through those tunes of his!"

I made notes as rapidly as I could. "Were you injured? Was he?"

"No, I wasn't, not as much as you might've thought. It was mainly scratches and grazes. But I was very shaken up. I looked a real sight. My bike was damaged more than I was. William was fine. I didn't run into him. He just stood there and looked down on me like I'd fallen out of the sky in front of him, like it was all part of a show put on just for his benefit. That seemed to go on for ages. It was probably just a few seconds, that's all. Then he knelt down beside me and checked that I hadn't broken anything. He took off his overcoat and covered me with it. I was shaking and shivering with the shock. My cap had come off, and he bundled up his hat and scarf into a sort of little pillow and put it under my head. Then he shouted for someone to phone for an ambulance. He gave this girl walking past two bob to run to a phone box and call 999. He came with me in the ambulance to the hospital and then got a taxi round to tell my parents while I was being cleaned up. My Dad had gone to work by then, so he brought my Mum back to the hospital after she'd phoned Dad's manager at work.

"Anyway, they kept me in the hospital for the rest of the day and overnight. Then they said I was okay to go home. When I walked out to catch the bus, there was William, waiting for me in his Bentley. He drove me home. On the way he said he felt guilty about causing the accident, and wanted to make it up to me. He invited me to dinner at his house the next night. He gave me his card. When I showed it to Mum and Dad they told me who William was. They always listened to the old Light Programme, so they knew him. Mum said he'd looked familiar when he'd come round in the taxi, but she hadn't wanted to say anything, and he hadn't either. She said she hadn't guessed that he'd be so handsome, when compared with photos in the paper. When I'd seen his address I was a bit disappointed. I thought he would've lived in a flat near Hyde Park or somewhere posh like that. But he had a house not so very far from us. Mum and Dad were happy for me go round there and see William. 'Giving the boy a damn good meal is the least he could bloody well do,' my Dad said.

"I walked all the way. William's house was in a very nice area. The garden was as well-kept and tidy as if it had just been planted. I thought it wasn't a very grand house for someone so rich and famous, but he must at least have servants to look after him. Well, it turned out he didn't. He'd cooked dinner himself—he was good—and served it himself as well. We drank what he said was an excellent wine, and he gave me old brandy afterwards. I said it was nice—I've learned much more about such things over the years."

"It was this house, wasn't it?" I said.

"That's right, the same place," Strande said. "And I've kept it in the condition that William wanted, too. After dinner William asked me about myself. There wasn't much to tell, and that's what I said. I'd left school, joined the RAF. National Service had ended by then, but I'd reckoned it was a good way to get a trade and have a bit of fun at the same time. I spent most of my time at Gatow, West Berlin. I learned about electrics and went straight into my job on the Tube. I told him it was a skilled and secure job with good prospects.

"What I didn't tell him was that I'd realised things about my nature since I'd been at school. I'd accepted it easily enough when I'd found out I wasn't the only one. I'd begun to explore and enjoy it. Berlin was good for that, and London. And it was swinging London in those days. What I liked to do was still illegal then, but if you were discreet—"

"The love that dare not speak and all that," I mumbled.

Strande nodded, but didn't smile. "Well, I quickly worked out what the situation was with William and he did with me. William was twenty-five years older than me, but Mum had been right—he was a fine looking man, and in great shape for his age. That's a laugh now, isn't it? We got on really well. He was really pleased when I told him I knew *Lines Under London*. I couldn't have helped that—it was often on the Light Programme back then. William invited me to dinner again the following week, and when I got to the house there was a brand-new bike waiting for me. It was far better than the other one. He said it was the least he could do. That was right enough, and my parents agreed.

"So I started going round to see William once or twice a week. I began to help him catalogue his collection of music and records, and to run errands and deliver messages for him, sometimes to places in central London. He was starting to turn into a recluse even then. He just didn't care to meet people much anymore."

"What did your parents think? What did people think about him having a much younger man around?"

Strande sat back in his armchair. "You know, I don't think William had any sort of reputation. He was always too wary, too cautious for that. He'd bought this house when he started making a bit of money. He wanted to recreate the surroundings he'd been used to when he was growing up. He said he always felt safe and secure at home even though the world was going to the dogs. William never spent his money on a bigger house or somewhere in the West End. He hardly ever went out and 'networked' as they say these days. Maybe that didn't help with getting his music performed, but it helped keep him on an even keel. He didn't throw his money around, but he was generous to me and all the good causes you know about— he kept a connection with railways, he really valued that. Maybe that was another reason he liked me. I think Mum and Dad had guessed about me, and were pleased that I'd met someone who they thought was a good influence, but neither of them ever said a word. They seemed glad I was having a good time. They liked it that through me they knew someone they thought of as a celebrity. William and I just stuck together. I was used to being careful—even with all the changes to the law, I was still illegal until I was twenty-one. I left my job at Neasden and went to work for William. I moved into the house. And I'm still here."

The tea had gone cold. Strande got up abruptly and went out to make a fresh pot. I jotted down as much as I could of what he'd said. When he came back I could see that he'd been crying.

"Sorry about that," he said. "I think I've become as reserved as William always was. My old mates from the '60s wouldn't believe it!"

"You've told me a lot," I said quietly. "I can come back another time if you'd prefer it."

He shook his head. "No, it's all right. I've never talked like this. I know you're really not that interested, but I'd like to get it all off my chest. You might not want to use any of it. And besides, I haven't started yet."

I didn't protest: Strande was right. But I wanted to hear everything he had to say.

"*Lines Under London* was William's most famous and successful piece," Strande said. "When I came to know him he'd been trying to work on something to equal it, if not be better and even more successful. He'd been thinking about it when he'd walked out in front of me. William used to say that I'd crashed into his life with such force that I couldn't even consider leaving it until he finished the new piece. Of course, he never did finish it.

"William was writing another piece with a railway and London theme. It was supposed to be more serious than just a light orchestral piece, although he said he was using all the techniques and tricks he'd learned from the likes of Coates, Binge, Ellis, Toye, and all the others. And it would've been dedicated to Eric Coates. Later William said it would be dedicated to me as well. But it was taking him a long time to write. He was having all sorts of problems."

"What was the theme?" I asked. "What was the piece going to be called?"

"It was going to be based on the London main line railway stations. One movement for each: Paddington, London Bridge, King's Cross, Liverpool Street—all those places. There must've been about ten in all. One or two have gone, and they've all changed. You know. The music never had a formal title. The working title was *London Termini*. William usually called it 'The End of the Line'. He never lost his sense of humour. Anyway, just about the only time William would leave the house was to go to one of the stations and walk about, trying to get inspiration for the music. He'd put on dark glasses and a hat. You wouldn't believe it! He didn't want anyone to recognise him. Of course, not many people would've known him by then.

"William's problems with the music had started a few years before I met him. *London Termini* was to have opening and closing movements based on the Euston Arch. His first job was at Euston, and he remembered walking under the Arch every day. It was to be a grand and solemn tune at the beginning with the same theme used again at the end. William used to compose at the piano. I'd hear him bashing away at it."

"I've read about the Euston Arch," I said. "There was a campaign to preserve it when Euston was rebuilt."

"That's right. William had supported the campaign, but it didn't succeed. The Euston Arch was demolished in 1961, I think it was. William was disgusted by that. He said it was vandalism. And he always said that was why he could never finish writing the opening and closing sections of the music. I told him he'd think of another theme, but he said he never would. And then, the whole *London Termini* started to go badly. William liked to wander around the stations and look and listen, trying to stay unobserved. He said he tried to sense and absorb the characteristics of each station—and each was very different. He'd jot down a few notes or snatches of tunes in one of his books, and come home and work on them at the piano. Each movement was to try and capture the unique quality or personality of each station. You know, he used to think about how he would bring in birdsong somehow for the Marylebone section. He said Marylebone was the only terminus where you could hear the birds singing."

"That's true," I said.

"I don't know how William would've reproduced birds singing, or how he intended to make the orchestra play them. But he would've thought of something. Anyway, William said that the demolition of the Euston Arch had sabotaged his plan. It was like he was a painter and his model had lost an arm. William kept on talking about abandoning *London Termini*, but that wasn't his style. And it was as if he couldn't let it go. More likely it wouldn't let *him* go.

"Not long after I moved in William came back from one of his trips to the end of the line, as he called them. He looked ill. He said that he'd been strolling around Waterloo Station. He'd got a tune in his head and had sat down to write it out before he forgot it. Then he heard someone whistling it, and it went straight out of his head. Completely vanished. He forgot it, as if he'd never thought of it in the first place."

"Someone whistled the tune that Winter himself had just thought of?"

Strande nodded. "That's it. That's what William said. I asked if he'd actually whistled the tune himself and thought it was someone else, or if someone else could've heard him whistling and then taken it up. He insisted that he had the tune in his head and then someone else had whistled it and stolen it from him. A few days later he went to Broad Street Station. When he got back he said the same thing had happened. A theme had started going through his head. He'd started to hum it to himself, not loud enough for anyone to hear. Then a City gent in the full get-up walked past, whistling the tune. I asked

William if he could hum it for me or write it down, but he shook his head. He said he'd totally forgotten it. After that every time he went to a station and started to compose a tune, someone hummed or whistled it out loud. William said it was like someone or something reaching into his head and stealing his most valuable treasures or secrets. He drove himself into a depression. He couldn't do any work on *London Termini*. No other music either. It got to the stage where he tried to distract himself so he couldn't let himself think of any tunes. He thought that whatever it was that was happening might stop, and if he didn't think of any tunes they would all then come back, flood into his mind. William became even more reclusive and very dependent on me. I couldn't let him down. It was a terrible thing to see—William was much younger then than I am now.

"I offered to go with him to a station, so I could see for myself what happened. That enraged him. William said that I didn't believe him, that I thought he wanted an excuse for not writing any new music. Well, I'd never known what to make of what he told me, but I'd always tried to be kind and helpful and attentive. That's love for you. And later he said he was sorry.

"William did still occasionally go out and meet up with one or two very old and close friends. I think they were from the entertainment business. I never asked who they were, and it happened so rarely. I didn't know whether or not he'd ever told any of them about me. He probably hadn't, given the law and his caution with exposing himself to the possibility of any trouble. He always said he was protecting me, although I didn't feel that I needed his protection, and that I could look after myself. William still kept in touch with the manager of the first cinema where he'd been organist. I'm sure the cinema has been pulled down now, or converted into flats or something. I drove William into the West End and dropped him off at his club. I saw him go in, and then the old boy who he was meeting for dinner. We'd arranged that I'd come back in a couple of hours. Because of the traffic I decided not to drive all the way home again, but to park the car and wander around. I remember it was a lovely evening. I strolled around Soho and had a couple of drinks in some places I knew. I even met a few of my own old mates, although I didn't tell them what I was doing. But I think they guessed I was 'with' someone, because I was wearing a really smart new suit, the latest style.

"I went back and collected the car, and drove to William's club. Right on time he came out and got into the car. He said that he wanted to try going to a station one more time. I was to drive back home. He patted my hand as it rested on the steering wheel. I remember that because William never showed any sort of affection in public. He always said he thought it was too risky.

" 'Which one are you going to?' I asked.

" 'St. Pancras.' Then he walked away.

"On the spur of the moment I drove up to the top of Gray's Inn Road and parked the car in a side street. I hoped that nothing would happen to it in that area—some of it was quite dodgy then."

"Still is," I whispered.

Strande continued talking. "I was sure that I'd get there first, especially if William was going to walk all the way. I stood around the main entrance keeping my eyes peeled. I probably looked quite suspicious, but I didn't care. In the end I saw him. He wandered up and down the concourse, looking up at that vast metal roof and then around him in jerky movements, like he was watching and expecting to be attacked. He bumped into people a couple of times. I tried to get closer without him spotting me. William went and stood against the wall, leaning back on it as he dug around in the pocket of his overcoat for his book and pencil that he always carried there. He was just about to write something down when the loudspeaker started to crackle. There were announcements all the time, but this one felt as if it were going to be different. I can't properly explain it—it was as if all the air in that huge echoing space was starting to vibrate from a silent bell that hadn't been rung yet. I braced myself for the announcement, but nothing happened. The crackling went on, and I heard muffled talking and the sound of something being dropped on a hard surface. Suddenly everyone in the station seemed to realise at once that a microphone had been switched on by mistake, and prepared themselves to laugh at whatever they were about to hear. I glanced at William. He had his eyes closed, pencil still poised over his notebook. Then the air was split by a burst of whistling coming from the loudspeaker. It was only a few notes, but they formed a definite melody. A moment later a lad standing next to me grinned and whistled it straight through as well. The whistling from the loudspeaker stopped as suddenly as it'd started. There was a gulping noise, and the rustling was cut off, replaced by total silence. As people laughed or joked with their friends, I saw William had dropped his paper and pencil, and was sliding down the wall and onto the dirty floor. I ran over to him and made sure he was all right. A woman fetched a glass of water from the café. I told her William was my uncle and had fainted. As soon he was okay, I led him back to the car. We drove home. William never once asked how I happened to be at St. Pancras. And he never did."

A bottle of whisky had appeared on the table, and I nodded when Strande offered me a glass. The heavy crystal tumbler was reassuring. It was something I could feel and grasp. It was hard and real, not abstract.

"That's about it," Strande said. "I don't think anyone ever knew about *London Termini* except for me. Maybe he told one or two people that he was writing something with a railway theme, but that never got mentioned anywhere, as far as I know. I'm sure no-one else apart from me ever knew why he never actually wrote it, let alone why it was never published or performed. William destroyed all the notes and odd drafts that he'd been able to do before—well, before what I told you happened." He swallowed his whisky and filled his glass again. I turned down a refill. "That was just about the only thing that William did throw away," he said. "You saw the garage."

We sat in silence for a few minutes. "Do you think there'll be a revival of interest in William's music now he's dead?" Strande asked.

"Quite possibly. That's the way it seems to go. I promise I'll write a good piece. It'll do Winter justice. And I won't mention *London Termini*."

"I don't think I'd mind if you did," Strande said. "Except that everyone would think William had been ill and that was why he wrote so little during the last forty years. He was never ill. He did try to write a different type of music. You didn't see any of it earlier. No-one knows that Britten once asked William to set some poems for the piano. Can you believe that? I think they were by Auden or Day-Lewis, someone like them, from that time. And William tried to. Ben liked what he did, but William said he just couldn't quite finish them, and never allowed them to be performed. They weren't ever published. His last music, his last songs."

"And you still have them?"

"Oh yes. They're in the archive. You know, I could never sell this house and move away, not now, but I've been thinking. I could give all that paper and all those records away. I wonder if I should set up a formal archive of William's work and collection, or donate it all to a light orchestral music archive, if there is one. There's probably a lot of rare stuff. William used to say that the BBC and music publishers threw out light music by the hundredweight. That got him annoyed! Maybe your article will be good publicity."

"Maybe it will. I hope so."

Strande stood up. "Well, I've talked enough. You know where I am if you want to know anything else. Now I must water the lawn at the back. This place doesn't look after itself."

"Just one more thing," I said. "Exactly *why* couldn't Winter finish any more music? You never quite explained."

"It's simple, really. William felt he'd been attacked and violated. He'd attracted attention. He felt guilty, as if he'd provoked something. He thought that something had turned on him. So he didn't want to draw any more attention to himself. He was scared to."

Searching online I located a CD box set of light orchestral music that included a couple of Winter's pieces, including *Lines Under London*. I listened to it a few times while trying to complete my article. The owner of the light music website who'd first put me in touch with Strande emailed me to say he'd enjoyed it, and thought that I'd caught something of Winter's character and how it came across in the music. Of course, I'd used hardly anything of what Strande told me.

Apart from when I sent him a copy of the published piece, I never contacted Chris Strande again. He never acknowledged the article, and I never wanted to make the journey back to that house and garden where Winter and Strande had kept themselves in line, voluntarily or not, and where time had been kept on track, channelled and dammed until it had almost stood still, and where there were rooms stuffed with paper that could not communicate what was behind the marks and words imposed on it. I was curious about Winter and Strande and their whole setup, but not that curious. Not even after what Strande had told me. Unanswered questions can lead anywhere or nowhere. Partially answered questions can be even worse.

And yet I still occasionally listen to *Lines Under London* and wonder where the notes and melodies go when they die away into silence, and where they were before they slip out into the air and become heard. How were they originally invoked and brought to life, and with what, if any, choice? The expression that a piece of music has achieved a life of its own now has a chilling ambiguity. Where do the notes and tunes go when the scores are ignored, forgotten, or thrown away? What happens when the music is no longer whistled in the street, or the orchestras are disbanded? How does the music live on, except in the diminishing minds of those who know and love?

Out to Sea

For as long as I could remember I was aware of the islands. I could count and name all six in the straggling chain: Folta, Zhara, Ghrau, Ghelp, Laxalt, Riexa. Throughout my childhood and adolescence I never saw the islands, but knew for certain they existed. From time to time I recognised the islands as I gazed into a friend's eyes before drowning in them, or in moments when he gasped my name and shivered in my arms as we embarked on a new voyage of discovery. I grew up into adulthood landlocked, but the islands shone just off the coast, shimmering in the sunlight and as unattainable as the sun itself because of the surging waves and swift, deadly ocean currents. The islands secreted themselves at the back of my mind like an obscure place once described in an old travel guide or delineated on a worn and much-folded map. And as long as books and maps were left lingering on the shelf, neglected and unopened, the islands too were serene, dreaming in a kind of neutral zone, always looming but posing no threats. The pale blue expanses on the printed page surrounding the islands were a part of my mental scenery too, with any possible power to threaten or even just influence rendered all but void.

Over the years I told a few of the people I met about my interest in the islands. Some shared it, but most were merely sympathetic. I found one special friend who dreamed as I did, of the coast and the sea and of undertaking the short journey out to the islands. We discussed the visits we would make, reading and re-reading books and literature and gazing at maps and plans. We enjoyed tracing on paper the routes we would take and streets we would explore; even the names of the bars and restaurants we would visit and the wines we would drink together.

His mouth and his tongue, his sweat and occasional tears, tasted of the salt that we knew would sting our eyes as we walked along our beach, bracing ourselves against the warm wind off the sea. Sometimes we wondered what it would be like to leave our city in the interior and make a life on the islands. One night we decided to choose one island each to make our own. Friends sitting at the table with us cleared empty glasses and bottles out of the way, and I unfolded our map. We closed our eyes tightly. And when we stabbed down our fingers on the same island, we all laughed so much that people turned to stare. Although it had been something of a game, we were both relieved that we'd made the same choice. It was a further bond. Friends gathered round and congratulated us.

In the morning twilight I knuckled my own tears away again, rubbing them out of my eyes and licking my fingers. I grimaced as the sharp taste stung inside my mouth. "We are natural islanders," he used to say. "I know it. The coastal towns are lovely, but there's the strait to cross." I had been alone again for some while before I finally resolved to take the opportunity to get close to the islands and see them for myself. One day I opened a dusty suitcase and carefully took out and unfolded the map I found under a mass of outdated guidebooks. The map split itself neatly along its folds, coming apart so easily that at first I thought I was holding several small maps instead of a single large one. But clear to see was the jagged, indented line of the coast, marked with beaches and bays and towns; and apparently so close inshore, the islands, strung out along the coast like sown seeds fallen on the stony edge of a field. The flat blue of the sea—the mere representation of it—churned and drifted as I traced with my fingers the line of brown and green smudges that was the chain of islands nested in their sea. My friends and work colleagues were kind and thoughtful. Not many showed surprise. They urged me to get away for a rest, a change of scene, to do some exploring. It would be no problem to take a leave of absence. I folded the map carefully away and started to make the arrangements.

I arrived in the largest and busiest of the coastal towns at noon on a hot and clear day. I stood under the shady portico of the railway station and prepared to venture out into the burning streets. From where I stood I saw the street leading down towards the bay, descending gradually through painted terraces of houses and shops. I had bought the latest guidebook to the town and its immediate environs, which included the three largest of the islands: Ghrau, Ghelp, and Laxalt. I had read the book several times and studied the maps intensely. Even before setting out from home I had planned my route from the station to the hotel where I had booked a sea-facing room with a balcony. As I strolled through squares and gardens filled with red and purple flowers, I already began to feel at home, as if I were returning to my native place after a long absence. I made my way towards the sea, down to where the promenade followed the deep curve of the bay.

My hotel lived up to expectation. I was courteously welcomed and immediately shown to my room. The young man who insisted on carrying my backpack for me unlocked the door and explained where everything was. With a smile he opened the double doors onto the balcony and indicated that I should step outside. He followed me and drew down an awning made from a heavy and rough-textured cream-coloured cloth.

"Why, this is a terrace, and not just a balcony!" I said. "Will I be able to eat my meals out here if I want to?"

He smiled again and nodded. I followed him back inside and gave him a silver coin. "Thank you."

I had pulled out my mobile phone along with my wallet. The lad noticed it and pointed. "That won't work here. In the whole town, I mean. Or over on the islands either." With a last smile he closed the door behind him and I was alone in my room.

The sky was tall and empty: I couldn't gaze up into any part of it without having to shade my eyes against the sun. Behind me the town flowed up against its hills. Pastel buildings, brick and stone walls, gardens and lawns—all spread out like a cloth, with one bite taken out of it as if the sea had once risen up and swept away a crescent shaped section of land.

At regular intervals on the stone promenade there were wooden benches set under concrete shelters or canopies. I sat down and gazed over the beach and out to sea. It was calm at that moment. I had read that the tides were minimal, scarcely varying from day to day and season to season; it was the currents and surges that ran between the mainland and the islands that were the greatest danger. Their ferocity and unpredictability often made travelling between the towns and the islands difficult and hazardous. It seemed that it was impossible to swim to and from the islands: even though they were not far offshore, no-one who made the attempt had ever succeeded. Only a few visitors would now even consider trying. My book explained that there were no bridges, even though it would be possible to link the islands together like pearls, and then to connect the closest of the islands with the mainland. I found that daring engineering and architectural schemes had been proposed and planned, but there was no evidence that any of them had ever been started.

I had decided that there was no point in coming to the town unless I also actually visited at least one of the islands. I looked up and away from the people on the beach, and out to sea. Between the distant headlands of the bay, I could see the three local members of the chain of islands. Silhouetted against the hot sky and floating on the iridescent sea, the islands solidified themselves from coloured shapes on a map into living stone and soil. It seemed that none of the islands had any large towns or villages; their permanent populations were small and scattered, but when visitors did find their way over to the islands, they were welcomed and fussed over. I read that many permanent residents were visitors who had never wanted to leave.

As my eyes grew accustomed to the glare I made out several tiny black specks, bobbing up and down in the swell of the sea. Although large motor boats were used to transport supplies, equipment, luggage, and almost everything else deemed necessary for life to the islands, they very rarely carried visitors. Anyone wishing to make the journey out to the islands negotiated their fee with one of the many rowers who kept their boats moored at a reserved part of the quay at the bottom of some steps leading down from the promenade as they waited for passengers to ferry across to the islands.

At breakfast on my terrace I drank glass after chilled glass of freshly squeezed fruit juice. The previous night after dinner I'd wandered back out into the town and found my way to a bar in one of the squares, not far from the rowers' quay. I must've drunk nearly two bottles of the spicy red wine produced on the hills above the town. Towards the end of the evening a man who looked only a few years younger than me asked to sit next to me at my table in the crowded barroom, and I remember offering him my bottle to fill his empty glass. He accepted, and we started talking. He had done much more research than I had.

"I'm a visitor here, too," he said. "I'm going out to one of the islands tomorrow. Probably Laxalt, I think. At least, I hope so. I finally arranged my fare with a rower this afternoon. I've been longing to come here for years, and I'm longing even more to get out to an island. I'm not afraid."

"Why would you be afraid?" I asked, more to listen to his lilting voice than actually get an answer. "Why would anyone?"

"Well, perhaps 'afraid' isn't quite the right word. But wait until you look for a rower—your rower. It's strange. Although I've heard about the hiring of the rower and his boat, and the ferrying across, how it all takes place, I never really believed it. Once we knew, I didn't have to work at it at all, only to agree the fee."

"What if you hadn't?"

He thought for a moment, before draining his glass. "In that case I don't think I would've ever come to this town. You're here too, you should understand!"

We left the bar together and strolled for a while through the starlit streets and gardens, but I was alone by the time

I arrived back at my hotel. We must have taken leave of each other, but I couldn't remember everything. I had a good feeling about him and the evening, though.

Now, sitting under the creamy awning on my terrace, I drank coffee and ate warm rolls broken open and spread with soft cold butter. I glanced at the guidebook I'd put out on the table: I planned to read parts of it again, and I also wanted to use it as a conversation opener when the young man came back to clear the table and take away the remains of my breakfast. He smiled as he worked. I told him what I recalled of my conversation from the night before. As I watched him stacking plates on his tray, a memory of my friend clearing another table in another place and era pushed itself forward, and I reached out for his hand. At the last second I took the book instead. If the young man noticed, he didn't show it.

"I can tell you that fewer come back than are ferried out to the islands," he said. "I was born in this town and have been out to visit several times since I was old enough. It is visitors like you and the man you talked to who have to decide what to do and then hire a ferry for the right price."

I walked up and down the promenade above the rowers' quay. I tried to act casual, as if I were just wandering around, taking in the sun and the fresh salty breeze blowing in from the sea. But I'm sure no-one else on the promenade who took any notice of me would have been fooled.

I leaned on the marble parapet near the steps and gazed down at the quay. Then I noticed my acquaintance from the bar making his way carefully down the steps. At the bottom he looked up at me, shielding his eyes. I thought he'd seen me and was waving; I saluted him back. Perhaps I saw him nod and smile, but the sunlight was strong and I might have been mistaken. He walked over to where two rowers were standing by their moored boats talking. He spoke to one of the boatmen and they shook hands. My acquaintance handed the rower his suitcase and was helped into the boat. Then they rowed away from the quay. I followed their progress as the boat became smaller and smaller, before finally into a black dot which was lost against the bright green and brown of one of the islands. As I stood there in the hot sunlight I suddenly felt an empty yearning, as if I'd just lost another close and dear friend.

The rower who'd remained on the quay pointed at me, and when he saw that I'd noticed him, beckoned me down. He was slim, taller than me and much younger, wiry and muscular. He wore a white shirt unbuttoned almost to his waist, and with the sleeves rolled high up over his biceps. His skin was tanned by the sun, but looked smooth and clear: not the skin of someone who spent his working days outside in fresh air and sea spray. As we shook hands I felt his strength and the power in his arms.

"You want to go to the islands, one of them out there."

"I think so, yes."

"You do."

The rower looked me up and down. It was the old feeling of being flayed out of my clothes. My mind cycled through the usual imaginings. After long moments he smiled and nodded, and held out his hand again. I hesitated to take it.

"What will it cost?" I asked.

"What do you wish to pay?"

I did a quick mental calculation. If I left the hotel tomorrow, and then travelled straight home again after my return from the island . . . I named a sum. He nodded, and we shook hands again.

"Come here this time tomorrow," he said. "And you will find out if you wish to pay."

The rower turned away before I could ask what he meant. I gazed at his broad shoulders straining the fabric of his shirt as he walked back to the edge of the quay.

The next morning I packed my backpack and checked out of the hotel. The young man I'd seen on my first day escorted me out into the street. I felt like someone who had been dismissed and had to be shown off the premises. But he beamed at me and murmured something about hoping I'd had a good stay and wishing me a safe journey in the future. I wandered out to the rocky fields at the edge of the town until it was time to make my way to the quay and meet my rower. Below me, white and pastel buildings glowed in the sun, and the subdued buzz of activity floated up to me in the still air. I ran my hand over rough stones and felt the stored warmth seep into my fingers. I gradually circled back down through the crowded streets as the time of my appointment grew closer. The weight of the backpack slung across my shoulders was negligible: it felt much lighter than when I'd first packed it.

When I reached the promenade I paused at the top of the steps leading down to the quay. There were several boats moored at the quay, with their rowers standing beside them. Some were chatting to each other; others were talking to prospective passengers. A boat was just drawing away; for a moment I thought it was my rower, but then I saw him standing next to his boat by the edge of the sea. There was a young couple, a man and a woman, talking to the rower nearest the bottom of the steps. The man and the rower shook hands, and the woman started to cry and tug at the man's arm. Then, as he tried to get into the boat, she put her arms around him, trying to stop him leaving. He disentangled himself as tenderly as he could, taking his rower's offered hand to help him into the boat. I was about to walk down the steps when the woman rushed up them and pushed past me. She was distraught and sobbing. I tried to take her arm, but she shook me off and ran on across the promenade and disappeared into one of the narrow streets that opened onto it.

My rower took my backpack and put it down next to the single passenger seat. Then he held out his hand and guided me as I stepped carefully off the quay and into his boat. I think I could've managed without him: the swell of the sea was so gentle that it hardly seemed to be moving. But I couldn't decline the offer of his hand.

"Did you see that woman just now?" I asked.

"That happens sometimes. There can be children too, mainly the older ones. It's best when men arrive here alone. You are alone."

His tone of voice irritated me for a moment. How did he know I was alone? I swallowed, remembering. What did he care? Well, my rower almost certainly didn't care. He was going to do his job and fulfil his part of our bargain—that was all. I dug my wallet out of my pocket and counted out the fee we had agreed on. He took the gold coins without a word.

"You are in my boat—you must want and be able to bear the cost."

"What do you mean?"

"I will row you across."

"Yes, I know, but—"

"You are one of us."

My rower sat down in his seat and pushed the boat away from the quay. Then he took both oars and began to row, surely and steadily, out to sea.

The town was steadily shrinking into the horizon behind us when I realised that I didn't know which island he was taking me to. We hadn't discussed it or agreed anything. I remembered from my map that Ghrau was the largest; for some reason I'd always assumed that I'd go to that island.

"I've forgotten to ask," I said. "Which island are you taking me to?"

"Don't know yet. Wait."

"Surely I need to arrange somewhere to stay?" I didn't mention anything about a return passage. "I talked to a man who thought he'd be going to Laxalt. Maybe the rower who took him is a friend of yours?"

"Laxalt is a good place. Now do be quiet. I must find the current."

So far the sea had been as smooth as a sheet of glass. To my left and right (or, rather, port and starboard, I corrected in my thoughts, smiling to myself) I saw the sea and sky merging in a darker blue haze or mist. I turned to look at the islands. But they seemed no closer than they had from the shore. I couldn't tell which one we were approaching. And back where we'd come from I saw the sun-washed buildings and trees of the town, nestling under the line of brown hills rising behind it. The boat seemed to be hardly moving at all, despite my rower's labours and the gentle swelling of the sea. I wondered what he meant about finding the current. I thought that'd be the last thing he'd have to concentrate on.

Suddenly he began to row faster, and the boat started to pitch and roll, as the swell also increased. Spray started to fly into my face. For the first time I heard waves lapping against the side of the boat. My rower grunted with exertion and sweat dripped off his forehead. I found a handkerchief and wiped the salt water off my face.

"Don't do that!" he shouted. "You may swallow the sea, not wipe it away!"

The boat continued rocking in the surge. I began to feel a little sick. We were now going round in circles. My rower seemed to be making it happen rather than trying to fight it. Then I leaned over the side and vomited up what felt like every meal and drink that I'd enjoyed since arriving in the town. The sea swept the stinking stuff away and I felt better. I licked my lips and swallowed the salty water that blew into my face. The burning sensation in my throat started to ease, and I leaned over the side again to scoop up some water in my cupped hands. I rinsed my face and swallowed; as I did so I saw my rower grinning. He let go of the oars, and the motions of the boat calmed. My rower slid the oars out of their rowlocks, and pushed them into the sea. I watched him as if in a trance. Then he reached forward towards me and grabbed my rucksack. He threw it into the sea. It was carried away by a strong current that now ran past the boat, even as we seemed to be becalmed, motionless. The oars were swept away by the current as well. I opened my mouth but no sound came out. I couldn't form any words. Still grinning, my rower leaned forward again and grasped my forearms. His grip hurt. I cried out in surprise and pain. I swallowed more seawater.

"You can bear the cost," he muttered.

Then he pitched us both out of his boat and into the sea.

My rower embraced me as we slid beneath the surface. I swallowed freezing water, gulping and gasping, losing bubbling air from my lungs as I fought against my rower and the desire to scream. The water pressed in on every inch of my body, swirling around me and invading wherever it could. My rower still gripped me. I wriggled and fought, but couldn't loosen his hold. My clothes were peeled off me by my rower or by the sea. Then I was on my own. I thrashed around, trying to rise back towards the surface, but I couldn't make any headway against the current. The billowing silver sky above me tilted away and the water grew darker all around me. I swallowed more water; but now it didn't taste of salt and wasn't quite as cold as before.

I thought I saw my rower swimming away, slim and lithe, darting like a smooth fish. I couldn't remember how deep the channel between the mainland and the islands was; numbness closed in on my arms and legs as my head seemed to blow up like a balloon expanding out of control. I blinked again and again as a dark wall rushed up at me, and became a floor then a ceiling. My chest and head throbbed with pain. I think I touched bottom in a cloud of sludge and broken plants; debris swirled around my knees as I waded through the mud.

The water became steadily more viscous. Now I floated just above a smooth road, sand drifting across its white and red patterned flagstones. I glided past the massive bases of enormous broken pillars, the ruins of the bridges that once connected the islands with the mainland and long since thrown down and drowned. I still wasn't moving under my own strength. Once I saw a skeleton. There were a few gold and silver coins scattered around it in the yellow sand. I reached for my wallet, but my fingers touched nothing except slick skin.

My rower asked a question for the first time, and I answered: Yes. Air I didn't know I still held bubbled out of my lungs, up in front of my face as the silver sky rushed towards me and broke apart. The sun burst in my eyes, warming my wet body.

Dry hands, strong suntanned arms, rolled me over onto my back and then pulled me to my feet. I felt the pleasant sensation of fabrics against skin—my clothes were as dry and warm as the sand of the beach. I was led away from the sea endlessly throwing itself against the sand, too tired to care. They led me to where a flight of steps, cut into the steep rocky slope, ascended from the beach. At the foot of the steps, in the sand, a wooden chair had been planted.

My rower said, "Sit down." He placed my backpack next to the chair, easily within my reach.

I looked at my rower and then all around me. Two sets of footprints trailed back to where I had been lying, next to where my rower's boat had been beached just beyond the reach of the waves.

"This is Ghrau," he said.

A shout of welcome drifted down on the soft breeze. A moment later a man stood in front of me and offered me a glass of chilled amber wine. Condensation dripped from the heavy pale green crystal. I drank it gratefully.

And now I sometimes take the battered old guidebook down from its shelf, or examine the worn and fragile map of the town and offshore chain of islands. I count and name them: Folta, Zhara, Ghrau, Ghelp, Laxalt, Riexa. I drink the cold clear wine of Ghrau and look out over the silky sea to the distant town, its windows glittering in the sun. I remember the currents as well, and look for the rowers at work. Occasionally, when we welcome a new visitor, I carry one of my chairs and a glass of wine down to the beach. And I still remember my rower's words to me before he set off back down the beach and climbed into his boat to row back to the mainland: "You are one of us."

Time and the City

The city bears no name, or at least they have never been able to discover it. So it is the City. There is a map, but there are no names inscribed upon it. The precise material the map is made from remains uncertain. And it is not even possible to determine how it was produced: whether it was drawn, or printed by a process long since lost—and lost so long ago that the loss itself is not remembered.

From the start they are able to make out the course of the river, together with the surrounding hills and valleys, and the barest skeletal outline of the City. The lattice of its plan reveals itself: twining and intersecting threads of varying widths laid down over the charted landscape, the many forums, squares, arenas, and other spaces marked only by the absence of lines. Many of the City's streets and ways clearly take the natural paths of contour lines; others are part of a formal geometry imposed on the land, lines knotted together in an encompassing net that could catch anyone who chances to come upon it. That is all.

Kayler decides to dedicate himself to exploring the map and seeking the city it reveals. He experiences the icy exhilaration of gazing down into deep time—as he stares at the ancient city, contemplating it, he feels as if he is standing at the edge of an abyss. Layer upon layer of strata fall away before him as if tumbling with him into the millennia. At other times, as he concentrates on a particular area of the City, or a certain feature, it is like staring into a yawning shaft, a wondrous vertigo seizing him as the depths rush up to meet him, inexorably coming into resolution around him. To Kayler the nameless city becomes truly the only City. He sinks into the pit of time; he embraces and returns its chill grip.

He stands at what was once the centre of a world. Sunlight slants over roofs covered with golden tiles. Shadows grow long as the sun goes down behind the temples piled up against the City's low hills. Ahead of him, on both sides of Triumphal Way, rows of marble columns march towards infinity, striking into the empty sky. If the pillars were ever capped by statues, there are none left now. As Kayler strolls towards the Central Forum the procession of topless columns sow in him a sense of incompleteness and jeopardy: as if a gigantic knife has sliced a layer off the top of the City, and might sweep back again at any time.

Soaring above the Central Forum and crowning the City's highest hill is the Verdigris Dome. The metal flashes and glints in the setting sun. He starts to walk across the patterned red and black marble slabs towards the mighty staircase that mounts the hillside rising towards the Dome. Space opens out on all sides of him. During all of his time in the City he has met no-one, seen no-one. There is no sign of any life. The City seems deserted, as if scoured clean by the winds that gust in from the surrounding plains.

Kayler snaps out of his reverie as the train clatters into the station. From memories of wandering across the vast open space of the Central Forum, the Verdigris Dome swelling into the sky in the distance, Kayler recalls himself to the swaying carriage. Advertisements flash past on the tunnel walls. Soon he is standing on the platform gazing at grimy tiles. A fresh blast of warm wind pushes its way into the tunnel as another train roars towards the station.

Outside at street level Kayler smells the fumes and hears the rumble of traffic and the endless subdued muttering of the people crowding the pavements. He is jostled; he looks around him for the row of columns, but lamp posts are no substitute. Litter frolics around his feet. He hesitates, thinking that next time he will walk to a quay and get into one of the empty boats, but a train is crawling slowly over the first bridge he comes to, and the river is the wrong one. He shakes his head, trying to fully return himself to the present.

He thinks of the map of the City and how the River Mercuriel meanders through the grid of streets. So far he has crossed the river once, on the Segmental Bridge; he saw the ranks of boats tied up at the empty quays, and vowed to follow the slow and drowsy flow of the river from one side of the City to the other. He sits on a bench, feeling the solid wood pushing up in reaction against his weight. This time in the City he knelt on the terracotta paving of Three Fountains Square and had been able to feel the gritty material as he rubbed his palm over its surface. For the first time it was as if the City had declared something of itself to him. It isn't far to Melas's office.

He tells Melas that he is beginning to hear the sound of the wind and to smell the grass. "The resolution of the Bistre Quarter has improved significantly, then?" Melas says.

Kayler nods. "Yes. Triumphal Way is forming out well. It will be interesting to see if statues do grow on top of the pillars."

Melas smiles. "Couldn't you choose more evocative names? Maybe I should be more careful how I put you under, try and influence you while you're . . . away. Back there."

Kayler invents the names. Every street and building in the City on which a name has been bestowed is given it because it seemed right, because it seemed to fit. "Those names choose themselves," he says. "The map is filling itself in, isn't it? It wouldn't if the names weren't accurate."

"I expect you're right. Let me know when you want to look at the map again," she says softly. "If you think you really need to."

"Soon," Kayler says. He remains seated and closes his eyes. The City is there in the nebulous distances within.

He crosses the expanse of the Central Forum and stands in front of the Arch of the Dawn. The Forum's paving pushes up against the soles of his feet. Kayler feels the distance walked, and the slight ache increases as he contemplates the switchbacking steps rising from beyond the Arch as they climb the heights towards the Verdigris Dome.

If the orientation of the City is what it seems, the rising sun will shine directly through the Arch of the Dawn on the spring and autumn equinoxes. Shadows, miles in length, would be cast along the white marble slabs of the Avenue of the East, which is aligned precisely with a notch in distant mountains now becoming visible to Kayler for the first time. He breathes in deeply. The morning air of the City is becoming richer: now he smells smoke and the occasional tang of salt from the sea he knows is there. Under them there are traces of animal smells and a multitude of odours that can only come from cooking.

They become stronger, even as Kayler stands in front of the tremendous Arch breathing them in. He is alert for sounds, too. Surely they will soon intrude—or, rather, claim his attention as is their right. He imagines parades and processions converging on the Arch from the three broad ways leading into the Central Forum. He sees the glitter of gold and silver and the multi-coloured twinkling of gems, flashing armour and swishing robes and cloaks. He sees chariots and carts; elephants, oxen, and horses. In the silent morning Kayler hears trumpets and the steady beat of drums, matching the marching soldiers and the creaking wheels. There are shouts and cheers as the head of the procession passes under the Arch of the Dawn and comes to a halt. The very stones would be calling out acclamations in exultation.

Kayler walks into the shadow of the Arch and through the main portal. He takes another look around: still no sign of anyone, anything. Nothing moves. Then he spreads himself against the warm marble, its veins and flecks little further away than the ends of his eyelashes. He grasps and smells the building blocks of the City. His tongue flickers out and for a moment touches his condensing dream.

Melas asks him about the people.

"If I'd seen any I'd have told you," Kayler says. "But I can feel them more and more each time. The sheer depth of the past—our past, not theirs, of course—terrifies me and yet makes me glad. Can you imagine it, Melas? How much I've travelled in the City, how far I've penetrated into its secrets, yet still knowing so very little! I will hurt myself if I were to stumble and fall, now. There is the white and grey stone, the marble, the terracotta and polished wood, the cloudy glass and green bronze. And, yes, its people. The City, Melas, the City!" Kayler shivers. "And aeon after aeon! Now put me under."

Kayler slowly toils up the first set of the great ranks of steps. The Arch of the Dawn is behind and below him. He remembers the golden coffered vaulting of the main portal, and the narrow staircases channelled into the thickness of its piers, tempting him to climb. But he ignored the small staircases.

Reaching the first terrace Kayler sits on a wide stone bench that follows its course around the side of the hill. The hill now seems entirely encased in stone and covered with marble buildings. The colossal mass gleams in the sun and hurts his eyes. In front of him the City unrolls itself, a stone carpet flung out to the low ramparts of its surrounding hills. Kayler can easily see the Central Forum and Triumphal Way; the expected—or intended—statues are beginning to grow on top of the rows of columns. He sees the City stretching out over gently undulating land, covering its smooth rising and falling in a succession of frozen waves of architecture. Domes bubble and towers leap up from the dusty colours of the packed buildings below him. Kayler sees the glint of the river, its bridges holding the City together like stitches knitting a deep cut. The sun is a circular smear in a white sky, too bright to look at but impossible to ignore. Kayler absorbs its heat just as the City does. He turns away and looks towards the next section of the steps. From where he is standing the Verdigris Dome is hidden by the blinding ranks of pillars and porticos, pediments, towers, terraces, and row upon row of arches sweeping up before him. He starts climbing again.

Kayler rushes towards Melas's office. The pavement is crowded—the complete opposite to the streets and boulevards of the City, which remain deserted. The people around him, moving with the same tide as him, or weaving against it, are reassuringly solid. They cast shadows. They make noises. They touch each other and brush against him. Kayler thrusts his hands deeper into his pockets. Suddenly someone steps in front of him and asks a question. Kayler blunders on, straight into the man and past, out the other side. He still feels the contact, but it's like emerging from a stiff revolving door. The voice trails away in anger behind him. The crowd looks less substantial now. Kayler reaches Melas's building and bounds up the steps.

She tells him that the map now shows a definite wall girdling the City. "The City is almost circular, as if it was built at the centre of a shallow saucer hundreds of miles across. Is that how it really seems?"

"Yes," Kayler says. He prepares himself to return.

At the next terrace Kayler turns and surveys the City again. He gasps at what he sees. In the Central Forum and boulevards feeding into it there are now hundreds—thousands—of minute specks. Some are moving, milling around each other; some are still. Kayler blinks several times, in case the spots are inside his eyes. He shakes his head in wonder. There are boats on the River Mercuriel—small craft showing tiny squares of sail. The City's people are returning.

For a moment Kayler considers descending again, but in his experience so far when something has resolved itself into life, it remains. The people will still be there when he comes down from the Verdigris Dome. Kayler lets his gaze linger on a grid of streets and open spaces nestling close to the wall, and distorted due to his angle of sight and the distance. The area is bisected by a canal, which leads straight towards an enormous arena or open theatre in the centre of—he decides to name the district Sunline. Even as he does so its resolution sharpens and he sees its inhabitants strolling along the wide pavements or sitting on stone benches built into the embankments of the blue canal. He hears the thin buzz and flutter of conversation and laughter. Wheels rattle. Children run across an open space emerald with grass and trees. Flowers blaze out in their beds next to the yellow and white marble pathways. Melas will be pleased. He smiles and turns away, back to the waiting heights.

Kayler ascends stairway upon stairway, crosses terrace after terrace. As he gets higher the air grows thicker; he tastes it with every intake of breath. Columns of smoke rise from innumerable chimneys, and he smells the bluntness of stone warmed by the sun. Some of the buildings soaring above him now have windows instead of porticos. The crystal glass flashes in the sun and reflects the tall cloudless sky. Kayler imagines jumping up into one of the half acre windows and feeling it sucking him in, drowning him on the other side. When he tilts his head back the cupola crowning the Verdigris Dome is just visible above the terraces and pediments mounting up in front of him.

Two great stairways carved from what looks like a single piece of pale pink onyx curve away from either side of a pillared archway. Kayler walks towards the shadowed entrance and stands in front of a vast pair of doors sheathed in copper and worked with an intricate design of curving incised lines picked out in brass and silver. He reaches out and touches, only lightly, one of the large circular bosses or studs raised at head height on the inner edge of each door. Without any sound the doors swing open smoothly, blossoming open in front of him and drawing him onwards.

Melas frowns at him. "I heard them shouting at you in the corridor," she says. "What were you thinking of, Kayler? Why were you so rude and thoughtless? This isn't like you." She looks at him closely. "And you almost walked into me just now. Don't you see us?"

"I rise up through the millennia each time you bring me back," Kayler says. "This city and all of you . . . all of you . . . are like so many misty figures. Soon I will sink down into the pavement and be able to put my hand through any wall I choose. I pull the years into myself every time you put me under to go back to the City. I am years, decades, centuries—whole epochs—they stack up like the palaces and obelisks ranged around Gold Glory Hill. The magnificence of the City, the magnitude and power of its achievements! And that's not all, Melas. For the first time I glimpsed the machines.

"There were immense mechanisms, or maybe they were all one great sublime machine. It was all acres of glittering steel and shiny brass, with its own sets of staircases and balconies where there were switches and levers made from crystal and ivory and ebony. There were rows and rows of light twinkling and sparking inside jewels of a million colours. There were mirrors and lenses. And it rose up from the floor of the hall as far as it could go. You should've seen the size of the base supports and the flying buttresses of dull iron that held it all together. They were massive from where I stood and yet I think they were the best part of a mile below. And the sunlight poured in through the windows, and everything was warm and solid, with a heft and a—a purpose that made me shudder."

"Surely you couldn't know what that thing was for? What it was doing there."

"Oh, that's just it," Kayler says. "Yes, it *endures*. There was a raw purpose and power locked in those shining tubes. But I didn't—I don't—know what it is, what it's capable of. But it's stupendous—and so very old. I felt the air vibrate with something like the deepest note of an organ, almost too deep to hear, but not to feel, trembling at the border of my senses. Even the City itself is a modern suburb of boxy houses when compared to that machinery in that hall. Something, some power, is chained, kept in check. And I don't know whether that's by the machine, or for it—something hoarded for release through the machine. Oh, Melas, I'm sure those forces could tear through the ages, rip the world apart from then to eternity as surely as I could pull that new paper map off the wall and shred it into a thousand pieces."

Melas gets up from her chair and starts to play with the single plain gold ring she wears. She paces up and down in front of the wide window. "That must be the reason for the symbol that's appeared in the middle of the map of the City," she says quietly.

Space, enormous empty volume, explodes around Kayler as the copper doors open and he walks forward. A marble balustrade appears in front of him, forming a low barrier around the intricate glittering structure thrusting up from the centre of what he has always imagined to be a domed hall. Kayler thinks the object is a sculpture. Then he realises he is standing on a gallery, halfway up the inner surface of a perfect sphere like the inside of a small planet. Although it must be hundreds of feet away, at least, he sees the sculpture is clearly a mechanism. It thrusts on up past him towards the distant curve of the hemisphere suspended above. Something catches his eye: a ring of jewel-like lights is now flashing, with no apparent set sequence and at an increasing speed. The lights encircle a burnished metal depression, at the centre of which is a sphere of delicate silver, woven in a web. His eye moves to set itself on something that seems to be revolving or oscillating inside the silver sphere. With a shock Kayler realises that it must be a minimum of a hundred feet across. But he cannot quite follow whatever it is that moves; the motion of each full cycle is always interrupted, fading out and reappearing again in its orbit. He cannot tear his eyes away either. They follow the motion: a flickering like a bird imprisoned in a cage and fluttering in vain against the wire.

A shaft of sunlight lances down from the heights, channelled by mirrors into a waterfall of light. Kayler gasps as the radiant beam flows around the silvery sphere before being swallowed up inside it. The oscillations within continue, but his eyes ache violently from still trying to keep track of them. He feels his mind being pulled away, out into the void and towards the glittering web; at last he succeeds in wrenching his attention away and staggers backwards.

Eventually he is able to look up again, and notices what look like several narrow bands wrapped around the surface of the hemisphere, each progressively smaller in diameter the further away—up—they are. Kayler sits on the lowest step of a spiral staircase made of stone so smooth and seamless that it looks as if it were moulded in one piece with the colossal sphere. He gets up and continues his ascent, following the twisting way bored into the thickness of the dome.

The thin wind whips at his hair, which he pushes back from his forehead. The pale green of the Verdigris Dome drops away from where he stands, arcing down towards the City and its pattern of buildings and streets sprawling out so far below. The air is thinner and cooler; the sun seems warmer than he remembers from when he last stood on solid ground. The Central Forum is black with the mass of people crowding into the gigantic space. The streets leading to it are seething. Kayler knows that the inhabitants of the City are moving towards him in endless columns pouring like rivers of ink out of their streets, climbing towards him, following in his footsteps to where he stands. Now that he has reached the top of the Verdigris Dome, Kayler examines the white marble globe. The carved outlines seem familiar, but are certainly not the ones he knows, or thinks he knows. There is a globe on a stand in Melas's room; Kayler tries to visualise it clearly, but it wavers. The base of the marble globe is green metal, a baroque growth embossed with the symbol Melas had attempted to describe. He grips the metal railing. The faraway City draws itself into sharper resolution, names filtering out of newly-minted time. The City fits the map Kayler remembers. He dreads the memories of the awful gulfs separating him from the map—from all he knows. *There!* He is done.

Kayler reclines in a deep armchair in Melas's office, occasionally reaching out for the cups of hot sweet tea she has her staff making for him.

"Are you feeling better now?" she asks.

He shakes his head. "I will never feel better." Kayler looks around the bland and pale office with its window overlooking the busy street. Yet again he sees the rendered walls and wooden shelves, framed photographs and glowing computer screens. "Which end of the vortex have I arrived in?" he says. Melas leans in to hear.

"I knew I'd be lost if I let myself be taken by that—whatever it is—in the machinery, that *movement* in the silver sphere. Wherever or whenever it endlessly loops to," Kayler says. "It and the City are lost in the deep past, so far back that there's no physical trace left or even a hint in human memory now. But are they also lost in futurity, so far ahead that time itself is wearing out and allowing shifts we cannot imagine? Back then I raised my arms to the sun and the sleeves of an embroidered robe slipped back, exposing my arms to the light. I wore bands of silver and amber. The last things I saw were the map and the City as one, the muffled commotion, the first people reaching the place where I stood, when everything decayed like a film running backwards and the City toppled and shrank in on itself, the hills wore away, the river overflowed and spread out over the land until even that dried up and all became a flat plain. Somehow I saw all that. And maybe I will see it again. I do know one thing, though. Now we've found the City, it's always with us."

The Way of the Sun

James had set out from home with a single phrase echoing through his mind. It defined the purpose of his trip and the destination he longed for. *A balcony on the Mediterranean*. James assumed that he'd once seen a painting or photograph with that title, or perhaps it had been a book of travel memoirs. A balcony on the Mediterranean: it had become almost an obsession to him. It was an engrossing idea and certainly the place he now wished to find—or hoped would find him. He dreamed of fleeing out of the dank autumn into warmth and light. He drove south, travelling in expectation.

The new phrase came as a surprise. It was another that James couldn't remember ever coming across before, the origin of which was a mystery to him. He had thought that one phrase or slogan was enough to keep him going. Nevertheless, a particular moment passed and it was there in his head. As he drove, the phrase kept pressing itself into his mind: *the way of the sun, the way of the sun* . . . He soon added the capital letters, as the apparently haphazard group of words slowly gathered to itself the sense of a definite concept: *The Way of the Sun*. He recognised the kinship between his phrases. The new one was a companion of the first—perhaps the way to achieve its end. It was as if the Way of the Sun would be the means by which he could find himself a balcony on the Mediterranean. It became clear to James that he had something to search for, with intimations, hopefully, of something to travel on, whether physically or through some other mode. He certainly desired the sun—sunlight, the glare and glint, the heat—and all that he imagined went with it. He was even prepared for some inevitable shadow.

When he drove across the border into Italy and the main roads were labelled with a different set of letters and numbers, his feeling of expectancy increased further. He smiled ruefully. He imagined Andrew's voice, the casual dismissal explicit in every change in the tone of voice and posture of body—everything apart from his easy smile. "So now we have it: James's Way of the Sun. Let's look at all this in a little more depth, shall we . . . " Andrew would only think that he wanted to get away again. Andrew would have been right.

James headed towards Milan, where he'd booked a room for the night in a large and anonymous hotel. He scooped a selection of brochures and other leaflets from the table in the lobby to add to the newspapers he'd bought earlier, and went straight to his room. Although he had arrived safely, he knew that Milan was not going to be his destination. There was still too much of the north about it. He trudged along damp pavements. The city seemed to consist of too many wide and straight boulevards lined with high grey façades; there were none of the small squares, cobbled lanes, and white stucco walls that he wished for. He decided that he wouldn't spend the next day in exploring Milan's undoubted treasures, but drive on south. He ate dinner in the hotel restaurant and returned to his room.

As he got undressed he glanced at the leaflets he'd left scattered across his bed. One of them now caught his eye. It showed a wide, curving stretch of road sweeping across the landscape, with a brilliant blue sky above and jagged mountains in the background. Everything was sharp and clear. For a moment he thought that this couldn't possibly be an Italian road: it was completely empty of traffic—a perfect invitation for use by the motorist wishing to take a fast route to where he wanted his journey to end. Then his heart skipped a beat as he read the title AUTOSTRADA DEL SOLE. Highway of the Sun: a new road for fast traffic, a motorway, connecting north and south, from Milan to Naples via Bologna, Florence, and Rome. The brochure made it clear that most of the road remained yet to be built, but the vision was clear and enticing. He would still have to travel along the lesser roads following the rugged coast, and through the villages and small towns, as he'd originally intended. He would still be travelling along his own Way of the Sun until he found the place where he would stop.

James fell asleep and dreamed he was driving along the wide open road. On the Highway of the Sun there were no other vehicles; no cars but his. Low hills and fields with their solitary white houses flashed by. Then Andrew tried to grab the steering wheel but he fought him off. The roof was down, and Andrew climbed onto the boot of the car and waved as he jumped off. Within seconds James had left him behind, but could still see him in the rear view mirror. Andrew curled into a ball, rolling to the edge of the road. He got to his feet and dusted himself down, smoothing his hair back to its normal immaculate state, adjusting his expensive silk tie. Then he started to thumb for a lift, as he stood there at the side of the deserted motorway.

The weather was a return to summer except for the much shorter days. Rome was a city of dusty colours in the hot

October sunshine. The chance overhearing of a remark in his suburban hotel led James to abandon his original plans for spending two days in the city. He had been sipping a glass of very chilled Frascati in the bar. The couple at the table next to his were talking in English, and he had overheard the words "balcony of the Mediterranean". He hesitantly introduced himself to the couple and apologised for inadvertently overhearing their conversation.

"Pleased to meet you. Want to join us? The name's Johnson, Bill Johnson. This here's my wife, Joan. Just call us Bill and Joan, everyone does. Yes, the 'Balcony of the Mediterranean'. We know all about it. We've just come from there. There's this little town on the coast not far to the north of Naples. It's called Lamolfo. If you go there you'll see why it got the nickname. There's a particular stretch of promenade, where all that's between one side of the main square and the sea is a railing. There's a cliff, with a sheer drop. The views over the sea are stunning. You stand there and look out, and it really is like being on a balcony."

"Lamolfo isn't that easy to find," Joan said. "This big new motorway they're on about hasn't reached that far yet, and the main roads won't take you there. You need to take the small roads off the minor roads, if you see what I mean."

"We can show you on our map," Bill said. "It's in the car. I'll just go and get it."

"No, it's fine, don't trouble yourselves," James replied. "As long as I can remember the name I'll be all right, I'll find it. I'm not in any hurry anyway. I have a lot of time. I just want to drive south and let Italy do the work. I just want to absorb what Italy has to give: the sun, the heat, the light."

"The wine and the women!" Bill remarked.

James felt himself blushing. "Oh yes. Well, perhaps one of those, anyway."

Joan giggled and reached for her cigarettes. "We can help you out with the other. We know all about the other, don't we, Bill?"

The following morning James was eager to be on his way as early as possible. He hadn't slept well, and the dream involving Andrew had returned. And his offhand remark of the previous evening and the Johnsons's response still bothered him. He was relieved that his new acquaintances weren't in the dining room when he went in for breakfast. He had heard enough about their new car and the intimate details of their holiday to last a lifetime, let alone all the chatter about the Johnsons's other—arrangements—back in England. He quickly ate his rolls and drank his coffee, and continued on his journey. He tried to focus his mind on the Way of the Sun. Now he also had the name of a place to aim for, his balcony on the Mediterranean. He reflected that even if Bill's description turned out to be completely wrong or for some other reason the town wasn't suitable, at least he'd have seen and experienced more of Italy. He would've absorbed more of the hot sun and sharp light of the southern autumn. And he looked forward to some wine.

Once away from Rome, James chose whichever road seemed most likely to follow closely the intricate indentations of the coast. Whenever the road turned inland he regretted not having bought a map of his own and making sure of his route to Lamolfo. But the strong sunlight and warm breeze ruffling his hair brightened his mood and strengthened his resolve to continue driving by instinct. He had not put on a tie, and had even left the top two buttons of his shirt undone. Catching sight of his face and neck, now being rapidly tanned by the wind and sun, James smiled as he imagined the sort of comments that Andrew would have made concerning his casual attitude and appearance. As in the dream, Andrew would never allow any amount of heat to cause him to loosen the tightly-knotted narrow tie that he invariably wore.

Despite the ongoing lure of Lamolfo, James continued to drive leisurely. The twists and steep curves of the road, its sudden widening and narrowing, rising and plunging, and the unexpected revelations of vistas over the sea far below, all encouraged him to take things easy. The warmth loosened him. He stopped in small towns along the way and explored churches and villas. He sat under the trees in village squares and tried out his Italian on the locals. At tiny cafés he lingered over coffee and pastries, painstakingly reading his way through a local newspaper or poring over his guidebook. There were occasional signs of the construction of the Highway of the Sun, but he was content to follow his own way as he slowly travelled south. He thought of Andrew striding across Kensington Gardens, head down into the chill and damp breeze, holding his hat to stop it flying away with the rushing dead leaves, buttoned up in his overcoat and wrapped up by his scarf. James smiled and sipped a glass of chilled vermouth, shading his eyes against the hot afternoon sun.

The road passed through a small fishing village, forming part of a quay at the seaward edge of the main square. Although he was convinced that Lamolfo wasn't now very far off, James decided not to drive any further in the lemon twilight, but to find a room in the village and travel on to Lamolfo in the morning. He spent an hour wandering through the streets and alleys in the warm night. A dog snarled at him, and as he jumped back waving his arms at it, a torrent of what he assured himself must be the local dialect poured out of an open window above him. He found a room for the night, and after dinner strolled down to the edge of the sea, near to where he had parked his car. As he was checking that the roof was securely closed and the doors locked, he was blinded by the headlights of a car speeding towards him. He ducked down behind the bonnet of his car as the lights swept over him and were gone. He had the sense of a looming streamlined shape, menacing like a torpedo. There were windows with faces at them. As the rear lights disappeared into the darkness, he was sure that the faces and car had belonged to the Johnsons. He crept back to his room and went to bed. He left the balcony door open, and a warm breeze off the sea flowed into the room.

The life of James's dream flowed on seamlessly from the new dream of his life. His room was bathed in sunlight, the low and cool orange light of an autumn dawn. The heat mounted as the morning advanced. As he drove towards Lamolfo he scanned the road ahead for any sign of the Johnsons's car. Although the route was a tortuous one, it didn't seem to be as difficult or obscure as Joan Johnson had implied. When he finally arrived in the town he felt a renewed thrill of expectancy. He could smell the sea over the odours of cooking and the produce set out for sale in the market. He left his guidebook in the car, together with his jacket. He rolled up the sleeves of his white shirt. All the streets in Lamolfo seemed to slope down gently towards the sea, where the sky seemed larger and deeper than it did above the mountains behind. The light reflected off the white stucco of the buildings bruised his eyes, but he didn't put on his dark glasses. He wanted to see the town unmediated. James's command of Italian had improved, and he asked the way to the main square. He realised that he'd probably find it easily enough by simply allowing the pull of the streets' leisurely incline to do the work; but he imagined Andrew taking so long to recall details of gender and case while framing the question that his own much less polished but spontaneous and enthusiastic request would've been the one to gain a ready answer with approval.

Soon the main square lay in front of him, bathed in hot sunshine that seemed to owe more to high summer than to autumn. He stood on the lowest step in front of the baroque church, its tower rising into the shining sky behind him. The square seemed to be empty; there was hardly any movement apart from the islands of flowers nodding in the soft breeze. Even as he looked, they grew still as the breeze died away. Pavements and walls glared. All he could hear were snatches of music from radios, the sounds drifting out of windows which were black squares in the walls. And from far away and deep below he heard the sound of the sea: the swell of the water piling up against stones in the unseen harbour and breakers foaming on rocks. The two sides of the square on either side of him narrowed in front of him, channelling his progress towards the empty fourth side of the square. The bulk of the church couldn't provide a balance anymore. He walked on. Heat rose from the stones. The doors of the shops and cafés and houses were closed, their windows securely shuttered. All life in Lamolfo must be behind closed doors. The tinny music faded into silence.

James stood and stared at the line of railings, the elaborate whorls and circles of the design straining his eyes. He strolled across the road and stood at the railings. He took a deep breath and stretched out his arms in front of him, taking a final short step and placing his hands on the top rail. The metal was hot; the paintwork rough and scabbed, with patches of rust erupting through. He stood on the balcony of the Mediterranean. He was filled with the thrill of space, out there in front of him, out there above and below, as the sky and the sea met in a haze that seemed to him to contain all possibilities. He gazed into the haze of blue and grey that he remembered as the sky in Andrew's eyes before they changed and went clear and hard. He braced himself for the inevitable comments, but none came to break the silence of the heights. To advance out into it . . . His chest swelled as he breathed in the warm thick air. He tasted salt, and then the scents of wild herbs and flowers, of hot soil and stone—he absorbed them all as he stood gripping the railings of his balcony.

"Hey! Jim! Jim! It's us—Bill and Joan! Remember?"

James opened his eyes and saw his acquaintances from two days ago staring up at him. "You lazy boy, Jimmy!" Joan screeched. "Still in bed! Woke you up, did we? What were you up to last night?"

A few minutes later James stumbled outside in the hot sun. He stood with the Johnsons next to their car. "How . . . Why are you . . . ?"

"We figured we'd better follow you to make sure you found Lamolfo all right, isn't that right, Joan?" Bill said. "Took us a while to track you down, but we found you, didn't we, Jim? You can't get away from good old Bill and Joan! You could end up anywhere, driving on these roads. When the motorway's open it'll be better, but you know what these countries can be like. It could be years yet. Me and the wife, we thought we'd be good neighbours. Englishmen abroad, and all that, eh, you know, Jim?"

"We thought we'd be nice," Joan said. "We've already been there, you know."

"Yes, and we want to make sure you get to sample the wine and—"

"The other," James whispered.

The Johnsons broke into howls of laughter. "You boys," Joan said. "That's all you can think of!"

"Get ready, then, Jim," Bill said. "Let's go!"

James still felt dazed. He rubbed his forehead. His white shirt glowed in the sun, dazzling against his tanned arms. "No, it's all right, I wouldn't want to trouble you . . . "

"No trouble," Bill assured him. "Just follow us. We know the way."

The Johnsons's car was a long way ahead. Through the clouds of dust James noticed a sign for the Autostrada del Sole. He swung his car to the left and followed the side road, which soon passed over the motorway on an unfinished concrete bridge. James followed the signs, but it seemed that the road wasn't going to connect with the motorway after all. It ran parallel to the Autostrada del Sole, unreachable below him in unfinished cuttings or above on embankments with no way up to them. He choked in the dust. When he could glimpse the motorway, he saw that the surface was rough and only partially finished; it couldn't be driven on by any ordinary car. And there were never any construction workers to be seen. Bitterly James realised that he wasn't only throwing away his chance to stand alone at his balcony on the Mediterranean, but that his Way of the Sun was leading him to an endless round of banter and jokes with Bill and Joan Johnson. He wouldn't be able to escape them. He had wanted Italy to absorb him, and instead he had turned his back on it and yet again denied himself.

The road curved away from the motorway, and rejoined what was probably the original road he'd been on while following the Johnsons. He drove on for a few hundred yards before pulling over. He switched off the engine. In the distance he heard a car approaching. It bore down on him; the sleek shape flew by on the rough road, scattering pebbles and dirt in its wake. The faces of Bill and Joan Johnson grinned at him. James got out of the car and leaned back against the door. The metal was hot, burning the backs of his thighs through his thin trousers. He rolled back the roof and grasped the top edge of the door. He wished it were the railing in Lamolfo, on the cliff overlooking the Mediterranean: his balcony. He closed his eyes and remembered the warm vastness as it had stretched out in front of him, all but surrounding him. To advance out into it would be to—what? Eyes still tightly shut, James turned away from his car and put out his arm, thumbing for a lift.

The High Places

Averill Turner? Yes, I knew him quite well, probably better than most. He used to put up with me following him around London as he sought out interesting and obscure buildings, or kept an eye open for women who somehow intrigued him, and who he would ask to sit for him. Averill enjoyed painting nudes—almost always female—and was also much in demand for his architectural drawings: carefully composed and accurate representations of buildings or details of buildings. While I knew him I never once met any of his models, either at the studio or anywhere else. Averill rarely mentioned them. Actually, I only had his word for it about the women— he told me he liked to keep the two main strands of his artistic inspiration as separate from each other as possible. Later I did meet some of the people who'd sat for him, and they confirmed what he had said. They knew nothing about his architectural drawings. In these respects Averill Turner was two artists, not one.

Averill wasn't a stereotypical artist either. He didn't look much like one for a start—whatever artists are really supposed to look like. He was a tall, broad man—not fat, just solid bulk—with a face browned by the sun and wind of years spent outside in the London streets. He had a full head of fine black hair that he kept from flying everywhere with a navy blue beret. That beret was the only element in his appearance that could be said to belong to the stereotypical artist. He wore thick tweed suits all year round, only leaving off the waistcoat in the hottest weather. Averill certainly looked like someone who worked with his hands—which of course he did—but through the daily wielding of something much heavier than pencil, crayon, and brush.

I expect the rounds of drinks I bought in the evening after a day's wandering and sketching helped to ensure my continued welcome. But Averill didn't need anyone to buy drinks for him: by the time I knew him he could afford all the drinks he wanted. He just didn't like to drink alone. He remembered his early poverty and the sacrifices he had to make to pay for materials and a place to sleep and paint. Memories of those experiences never quite left him, and his generosity to a large number of younger artists was not as well-known as it deserved to be.

I can still visualise Averill's studio. It was a large room occupying most of the top floor of a house in a quiet square just off the King's Cross Road. I think the rest of the place was empty, although later, for reasons I'll come to, Averill bought a bed for one of the rooms. I usually saw the studio at night, and that's when I remember it best. There was no curtain or blind, and at night the window was like a black distorting mirror reflecting back into the room the lamplight and images of anyone who looked into its depths. Close up you saw the gleam of streetlights and the roofs of the other houses in the street falling away below. Averill worked at an easel, sometimes with a plain wooden chair in front of it if he didn't wish to stand. Other wooden chairs and stools were scattered around the studio on the bare wooden floorboards. There was a long, low workbench under the window, covered with pots full of pens and pencils, bottles of ink and pieces of charcoal. There was a cupboard whose doors were always swinging open, and which was full of tubes of paint, brushes, and piles of paper. Unfinished drawings were pinned to the beige walls. There were a few framed ones as well. The studio was usually very dim, except for where Averill was working or where his model was sitting. Then he'd rigged up ways of pooling the light where he wanted it and needed it to fall.

Averill produced several portfolios and had over the years been commissioned to provide illustrations for a sizeable number of books. There is one book by him that I don't have, and if you ever find a copy, snap it up or sell it to me! In 1923 Averill was granted access to the Bank of England—not the pompous monstrosity on the site now, but the elegant and matchless masterpiece by Soane— just before it was demolished. He spent several weeks wandering around, making drawings of endless halls, corridors, staircases, and courtyards, trying to catch the essence of the doomed building, the light as it penetrated the spaces and spread over the surfaces. In *The Old Bank of England Revealed* you can walk through Averill's drawings and into the crystalline and urbane world composed by Soane and his predecessors. Yes, when all's said and done, Averill Turner's work was as unlike that of the genius whose surname he shared as it was possible to be. I do agree that there was one exception, which I'll come to.

And Averill didn't only confine himself to the City and the inner districts of the metropolis. He had taken note of London's explosive growth, especially during the years following the Great War. He used to take a bus or trolley out to somewhere like Uxbridge or Ealing, walking to the edge of the expanding town to see the new districts springing up. Or he'd get off at a rural crossroads in Hendon, or in a hamlet which didn't even have an official name and where a hedge running alongside a ditch next to a pair of dilapidated cottages was all there was. He'd roam around the rapidly developing suburbs where the Middlesex soil was gashed, torn open, and overwhelmed by the coming tide of concrete, brick, and tarmac. Much as he loved painting female nudes, he also liked to take his subjects from other sources. He sketched the construction workers on the Great West Road and North Circular Road, and enjoyed drawing the new industrial areas, offices, cinemas, and Tube stations. Averill liked to draw these as much as he did the towers of Sir Christopher Wren's churches, and it pained him that so few people were as interested in them as he was. I hope that will change.

In 1938 Averill was commissioned to provide the illustrations for a magnificent two-volume study of the churches of the City of London. That was *Churches of the Old City*. Such a valuable assignment—both in the payment he was to receive, and in the service to posterity it would perform—can scarcely be imagined. Although the project was nowhere near complete at the time the Blitz started, many of Averill's drawings—and particularly the rough sketches—were unique evocations and records of places that shortly afterwards were blasted from the face of the earth.

The churches designed by Christopher Wren, and above all his mighty Cathedral Church of St. Paul, are still the glory of the City of London. Averill loved and valued the views of St. Paul's from Bankside or further afield. He told me that he saw the cathedral's twin towers and great dome soaring above the City, with the towers of the parish churches clustering beneath them, as the masts and funnels of a flotilla of small ships surrounding their flagship serenely at anchor in their midst. Averill revered the old engravings and photographs which, at first sight, portrayed a scene not changed overmuch from the days of Canaletto, although of course he painted London illuminated by a light that never was on our city. And it was a view that still remained easily recognisable right up until the 1950s.

What Averill detested was the gradual reduction of the number of churches. That was one of the reasons that Averill jumped at the commission. Wren's churches had been disappearing throughout the nineteenth and early twentieth centuries, usually as victims of road widening and other improvements to the aging structure of the City. Averill simply wished to preserve the survivors, to embed them more firmly and securely in the memory of the City. Of course, he would also be using his artistic talents and gaining financially in the process, but his main motive was creative, making a stand against the destruction of the previous decades and the threats to come. One thing we do know is the far greater menace that was shortly to engulf London and threaten all its treasures. When the serious bombing began in September 1940, Averill carried on as usual. During the day he sketched churches and towers, and then retreated to his studio to labour over the rough drawings and to shape them into work of a quality high enough to satisfy him and the book's editor and publisher. They were usually far more easily satisfied than he ever was.

Averill had bought a lovely Georgian house in Hammersmith, by the river. I remember him joking that he didn't want to live too far from Hogarth. And although it never figured very much in his work, Averill was as fascinated by the Thames as the other great Turner had been a century before. He spent his whole life within a mile of it. Averill was a true Londoner, as Hogarth and Turner had been. I think all three of them knew the secret of how to transmute London: they all felt safe there and were willing to get their hands dirty, and not just with ink or paint. As the weeks and months went by, Averill tended to stay more and more at his studio, making it the base for all his operations, rather than returning to his house to relax and sleep. Sometimes we still rode a bus or took the Tube out to some special place in a distant suburb, for him to spend a few hours sketching in clearer air and quieter surroundings. He was drawn to the heights. I remember that Sydenham to the south, Kingsbury to the north, and Horsenden Hill or Gladstone Park to the west were favourite vantage points. The vast pale carpet of London stretched out in front and below us. Averill would sketch a tree or some cloud shapes, and talk about a painting he hoped to do after the war: a vast panorama of London as seen from one of his beloved high places. As we stood on the summit of a hill, a sea of suburban roofs and parks lapping at its lower slopes, and netted by the new wide roads, he would point out the great buildings rendered insignificant and minute by distance and haze. Barrage balloons glinted in the sun, swaying on their mooring lines. Cloud shadows sailed over the fields and factories. In the incessant muted roar of the city and its millions, the great was rendered small and the canopy of the empty sky rose over everything.

There was one painting that did materialise from Averill's expeditions up to the tops of London's hills. That was *Now, My London*. It wasn't at all characteristic of his work. Instead it owed much to J.M.W. Turner—particularly the paintings the great man did of the Houses of Parliament on fire in 1834. Averill lived up to the truly "Turneresque" description in that respect. I once saw this painting on exhibition, and I remember that it was large enough to cover most of a wall. I can't think who ended up buying it and where it is now, but I'm sure it's at least mentioned in just about every book about Averill's art. He loved the views over London that you get from certain parts of Hampstead. During the Blitz he went there on several nights and painted the burning city, the view over a glowing, incandescent sea. In that picture London was at the heart of a silent volcano of flames. The city was transformed into solid fire roaring upwards in an inferno that could never be quenched. You might not believe it, but if you stood in front of it long enough you could hear the pandemonium of the throbbing of bombers' engines, gunfire, explosions, and the screams. You could taste the choking dust and the searing heat and steam in your throat. Hot colours burned and melted and mixed and swirled into each other. Luminous colours and shades of paint, textured streaks and whirls flew upwards in rising vortices tinged with silver and gold. There's hardly any sign of the night sky, the searchlights, flares, and bullets, the smoke-obscured moon. I always felt that walking past that painting was to take my life in my hands, to narrowly avoid being burnt up, consumed. You could feel the heat pulsing out of the frame, like standing in front of a furnace when the doors had been opened. I wish *Now, My London* were on public display now.

There were no respites for London—at least that's how it seemed in those days. Mr. Churchill might boost our morale by broadcasting on the radio, but the Luftwaffe still took to the air just about every night. In 1941 the first volume of *Churches of the Old City* was published, despite the restrictions on paper and printing. It was a great success among those lucky enough to see a copy. About half of the edition was still in the publisher's warehouse waiting to be distributed and got reduced to ashes when the entire area around Paternoster Row north of St. Paul's burned in December 1940. I'd never part with my copy.

Averill spent more and more time sketching and drawing. The possibility of getting caught out in air raids didn't deter him. Sometimes I accompanied him on these trips too, holding his bag of sketchbooks and drawing materials while he worked feverishly as the daylight faded. When the sirens went we would start thinking about heading for the nearest Tube station and the often tortuous journey back to his studio. Usually I left him there and went on home, but sometimes I stayed with him while he worked, checking the blackout curtains were properly adjusted, making cups of tea, pouring drinks, and generally tidying up and trying to make myself useful. I hadn't seen Averill on the day he died. For once he'd gone back to his house rather than the studio. And that was the night that Hammersmith got bombed.

It was only after Averill's death that the notion I've been beating about the bush in leading up to first occurred to me. The funeral had taken place at Golders Green—the irony was that Averill had wanted to be cremated anyway! I'd found the pale Italianate brickwork of the chapels and colonnades calming and comforting. I already knew the area quite well, and only a month or so earlier I'd accompanied Averill when he drew the Lutyens church and chapel just up the hill in the middle of Hampstead Garden Suburb. With the Free Church he'd spent a long time getting the steep gables and numerous dormers mounting up to where the dome burst out of them just the way he wanted to depict them. One moment he was roundly cursing the architect, the next pointing out an aspect of the brickwork or the massing against the sky as marks of genius. A few days after Averill's funeral I picked up my copy of *Churches* and travelled on the Tube to Golders Green. I strolled around the edge of the Suburb by the Hampstead Heath Extension. The spire of St. Jude's and the dome of the Free Church broke into the cloudy sky. I sat down on a bench and gazed at Averill's drawings, turning the pages slowly, at first trying to capture an overall impression of each building, and then returning to the illustration, letting each church, its tower or other details that Averill had drawn, come slowly to form and prepare itself for permanent display in the gallery of my mind. That sounds utterly ridiculous, looking back on it and now putting it into words, but it's the best I can do. There and then I vowed that one day I'd make a little pilgrimage to the churches that Averill had illustrated for the book. It didn't matter whether or not I'd been there with him when he'd done the preparatory sketches. I wanted to visit the churches again myself, for myself and in memory of Averill. It was as simple as that.

It wasn't until just after the war ended that I was able to fulfil my pledge to myself and Averill. The fabric of the City of London, woven over the centuries, was ripped and holed—a ragged blanket. Vistas were revealed for the first time in centuries. In the shadow of scarred splendour plants sprouted and flowers bloomed from the stones and bricks of shattered walls. I seemed to see everything from an unusual angle as if for the first time. I walked through my native city like a startled visitor. Although St. Paul's had been bombed, the damage had not been great. The vital thing was that the dome had survived. I tried to recall the inscription on Sir Christopher Wren's tomb, in the crypt. It's SI MONUMENTUM REQUIRIS CIRCUMSPICE, or something like that: *If you seek his monument, look around you.*

Since Averill had drawn them the possibility that some of the churches might've been destroyed or seriously damaged wouldn't make any difference: his drawings and paintings would be his monument, and I would do anything I could to ensure that.

I'm getting to the point, I assure you. I'd made a list of the churches that Averill had illustrated in the book. I was able to visit every one. They had all survived the bombing. Sometimes there'd been damage, but nothing that couldn't be repaired, and most important of all the towers still stood, a diminished crowd of sentinels surrounding the great cathedral at their centre. During the subsequent days I went through Averill's drawings. I'd moved them all from his studio and put them into safekeeping. They'd survived the war intact, every one. I made a list of every church and every other building that he'd drawn. And then I visited every single one of them. Yes, I know that the tower is often the part that doesn't get hit and survives. I believe that it is indeed very difficult to bring down a tower simply by bombing. I'm not making any claims. And yes, of course I know that St. Paul's was damaged. I said so. But it withstood the raids. There's that famous photo of the dome floating high above the smoke and fire of the inferno that engulfed the City. It did inspire us. And St. Paul's wasn't damaged anything like as badly as the Berliner Dom was. Did St. Paul's have better firewatchers? Was God with us and not with the cathedrals of Berlin? It wasn't me that used the word "miraculous".

Sometimes I wonder what Averill would make of London as it's become. He was never one to be stuck in the past. For all that he loved its buildings he never had undue reverence for it. The destruction by the Luftwaffe—the Blitz—sickened him, and I think that much that's been done in the name of renewal and reconstruction since, in the aftermath, would equally have disgusted him. But the Barbican, London Wall, and Route XI—the visionary and high quality schemes of London's future: Averill would've loved them and drawn them, again and again. I wouldn't have been surprised if he'd ended up buying a flat at the top of one of the Barbican towers and made his studio there too, if only he'd lived. If it had been an option, he certainly wouldn't have agreed with the detailed reconstruction of the old, vanished London as happened with the ravaged historic centres of some cities on the Continent. He hated fakery and dishonesty. You can see that in his paintings of nudes!

I do wish that Averill had once taken the time to draw his own house.

Me? I'm just telling you. I don't claim anything. I wouldn't dream of it.

Wandering Paths

By the time Vasile finished parking his car, he had finally succeeded in convincing himself that he had never been to Avrig before—let alone the Brukenthal Palace and its gardens. Although the town, with its main tourist attractions, was only twenty kilometres from his home in Sibiu, he was certain that he had never driven even that distance to visit them. He told himself that small towns in this part of the country all looked much the same, and that was the reason for any momentary assertions of memory. As he sat in the car looking along the main street he saw there really was nothing familiar. Possibly he had been unconsciously recalling photos and brochures that his wife must have shown him.

Vasile eased himself out of the car. For a few seconds he closed his eyes tightly against the sunlight hammering down out of the empty sky and reflecting off the dusty road. He leaned in and picked up his jacket from the passenger seat; but he didn't put it on. He made sure that his sunglasses were in his shirt pocket before slamming the door shut and locking it. Beads of sweat started to line up on his forehead at the hairline. Mirela had always been on at him to wear a cap or hat, if he insisted on keeping his hair shaved short. Not for the first time he wondered why he'd come to Avrig after all. He'd arranged to take a day off work, and could easily have kept the day free. He could now have been back in Sibiu, sitting under an awning outside one of the cafés in the Piaţa Mică sipping coffee, or in an air-conditioned bar drinking a glass of cool dark beer. But no: he was here. Shading his eyes Vasile crossed the road. He had parked as close to the Brukenthal Palace as he could. Even so, by the time he reached the entrance he was sweating freely. His shirt stuck to his chest and shoulders. He walked through the gate between the high central section of the palace and one of the two lower wings which flanked it on either side. Its roof was as steep as that of the main block, and the orange tiles flamed in the sun.

Mirela had suggested that they meet in the gardens of the Brukenthal Palace. She'd told him that the setting would be relaxing and would help to bring some calm into their situation so they could discuss it like civilised human beings before deciding what to do next. Vasile had barely been able to restrain himself from shouting into the phone that she'd already made up her mind. He had agreed to her suggestion that they go to Avrig. When he'd asked her where he should collect her from, she'd said that she would make her own way there. She gave a time for them to meet and described the place: a bench at the bottom of the steps leading into the gardens from the terrace at the rear of the palace.

When he'd received Mirela's text cancelling the arrangement and stating that there was no chance after all of her changing her mind, Vasile decided that he would drive to Avrig anyway. As he sat in the kitchen he'd thought it was possible that Mirela was testing him: if he turned up at the right time and in the designated place she would be waiting for him after all, and their marriage could have another chance. But even as the hope welled up in him he knew it was a false hope, and that he would be deluding himself. He struck the thought down. He opened a bottle of mineral water and drank most of it straight down, not bothering to pour it into a glass. He rubbed the chilled, condensation-covered bottle across his forehead and along his bare arms. He shivered for a moment. Then he drank the rest of the water and switched off his phone.

Vasile passed gratefully into the shadow of the palace and looked around for someone to collect his entrance fee, but there seemed to be no-one about and the silence of the morning remained unbroken. He saw a small wooden table covered with leaflets and took one. He folded a twenty lei note in half and left it on the table. As he walked out into the open court behind the palace he had an impression of yellow and white walls on either side moving in to enfold him. Glancing around, he became aware of the palace in its entirety, surrounding him on three sides, the old walls and roofs glowing in the sun. A row of tall and well-trimmed shrubs, shooting up like green flames from the hard ground, threatened to bar his way. Gravel crunched under his shoes and he was past the trees. The fourth side of the courtyard was open. A trellis fence supported by widely-spaced pillars formed the boundary. He strolled through the clotted air towards a gap in the trellis, framed by more trees, from where he could see the steps leading down to the garden.

Vasile ignored the wooden benches nestling on either side at the bottom of the steps. They were empty. So now he really did have the day to himself. The gardens stretched out in front of him, an unexplored territory. He folded the leaflet and crammed it into his pocket: he would do without the map. From his viewpoint he thought he could see everything. Two more flights of steps beckoned him downwards, onwards. The warm air was full of the scents of flowers and newly-cut grass. Vasile rolled up the sleeves of his shirt; his arms and wrists prickled with sweat. Hot and heavy, his watch cut into his left wrist, weighing down his arm. He slipped off the watch and dropped it into his pocket where it slid down to rest against his key holder and the map. He wiped his face and neck with his handkerchief before slinging his jacket over his right shoulder.

At the bottom of the steps was a pool. Its shape—a square intersected by circles—had been punched neatly out of the gravel. Clear, still water filled the pool almost to its convoluted rim. Vasile knelt down on the rough and lichened stone, warmed by the sun. He plunged his arms into the water, one after the other, up to the elbow. He cupped his hands and scooped up some of the water. It looked clean enough to drink, but he let it trickle back through his interlocked fingers into the pool. He gazed into its depths. The pool was probably no more than a metre deep, if that, but for an instant it held the infinite deepness of the sky reflected in the water. He leaned forward again and broke the glassy surface with his hand. The sky shattered into ripples, slowly subsiding and smoothing itself back out again. Vasile remembered why he was there, and loneliness returned, overwhelming his bitterness and anger. It would take almost no effort at all to complete the action and let himself roll into the pool, to strike down into its cool depths, to fall down and through it and dive into the sky and be lost. There need be no trace. No-one would miss him. He thought about their apartment, now almost completely drained of anything connected with Mirela. He swallowed several times and shook his head. He got to his feet and shook his head again. Tiny droplets of sweat flew off his hair.

There was still nobody in sight. The gardens seemed to be deserted. Vasile was pleased that he hadn't been observed. Ahead of him, on the far side of some fruit and vegetable patches, was a long range of single-storey buildings incorporating an archway that looked as if it would lead into another part of the gardens. The buildings had not yet been fully restored: the yellow walls were flaking and grimy in places, while in others the stucco had crumbled away. Some of the red tiles had become detached from the roof. He followed the path past the archway and a succession of white-framed windows alternating with stretches of golden-rendered wall. He came to an open door, and saw the notice scrawled on a piece of paper stuck in the window stating that refreshments were for sale inside.

The room was dim, and the air no cooler than it had been outside in the sun. The brick floor was uneven, and he stumbled as he walked over to one of the small tables and sat down. There were no signs of any customers. An empty mineral water bottle and a glass had been left on one of the other tables. A moment later a middle-aged man wearing gardening overalls came into the room and glanced at him in surprise. Then he asked Vasile what he would like. His first impulse was to ask for a chilled bottle of beer, but he wanted to keep his head clear. So he ordered a bottle of mineral water and hoped that it would be very cold.

The water refreshed him, and he strolled back out into the garden. It was nearly noon. The sun beat down and the light pressed in on him. He walked over to a stone bench that stood in the shade of a plum tree. He hadn't said anything to the man who'd looked at him so strangely, but the experience had unsettled him. When he'd paid for the water it seemed that the man had been about to make an observation, but he'd only smiled as he took the money.

He was in a part of the gardens that had been laid-out with great formality and was properly maintained. Paths and walks met at right angles or followed carefully plotted curves; beds of flowers and precisely-placed shrubs filled the areas in between. Small patches of lawn surrounded trees and symmetrically-positioned statues and sundials. Vistas were closed off tastefully. It dawned on him that there were many pedestals without statues, and yet they stood sentinel at the intersections of paths and flowering borders as if they were still whole rather than truncated. There were also numerous tree stumps thrusting up through the grass. A heat haze rose from the paving and the buildings quivered in the sun. Vasile felt thirsty again; his shirt and trousers clung to him. Stray breaths of wind stirred the trees, and the sounds of birds and grasshoppers subsided into a single hushed murmur. He felt that he'd reached some sort of peace. He wasn't sure now if he ever wanted to walk away from the gardens and back to his car, to drive home and return to his life in Sibiu. With Mirela gone and never coming back, he would have little reason to.

Eventually Vasile got up from the bench and wandered back along the path by the garden buildings until he came to the archway. He debated whether he should go back into the refreshment room and order a beer, but he didn't want to see the attendant again, or be seen. He stood in the burning sunshine. He transferred his jacket to his left shoulder, where it hung like a becalmed flag; he ran a hand over his head, pressing down the cropped hair, feeling the heat radiating from his scalp. On his right, through the archway, the gardens continued. On his left, the path led back to the pool and the steps up to the Brukenthal Palace, Avrig, his car, and all the way he had come. He looked back in that direction, screwing up his eyes against the glare of the sky. He patted his shirt pocket, rediscovering his sunglasses. But he left them where they were.

Fragments of red roof and yellow wall flickered through the trees behind him. Now Vasile was beyond the formal part of the gardens. A broad path ran on ahead, under trees. He was glad of the respite from the sun. He gazed out from under the trees at a landscape drenched in strong sunshine as if through the window of a shadow-filled room. Instead of being paved or gravelled, paths had been scythed through long grass—wide and ragged-edged, soft and yielding underfoot. Here the garden had turned into a meadow. He strolled along winding paths through the hissing grass. For a few metres the path he had chosen ran alongside a narrow brook. He came to a row of trees, which turned out to be an avenue leading away from the garden buildings. At the far end of the avenue, in the distance, Vasile could just make out the shape of an arch or gateway, which he thought must form the boundary of the estate. It seemed to be a very long way away down the dark tunnel of trees.

He looked for somewhere to sit down, but there were no benches by the paths. Wherever he looked, the air trembled in a heat haze. There were specks swirling in the air—or perhaps they were circling behind his eyes. There was a sudden movement on the path in front of him, where it joined another path. It was as if someone had peeped out from behind one of the trees there, and then jumped straight back. Vasile couldn't see anyone. He turned round. The path behind him was empty, but he was sure that someone had been there a moment earlier.

He started to sweat heavily again, feeling it trickling from his armpits. His forehead was wet and the salt sweat stung his eyes. He blinked away more of the dancing specks and blotches. Now they were like small black birds skimming the grass low in front of him. He stumbled on a small patch of rough grass and lurched onto another path. He found himself at the edge of a lake. It couldn't have been a large lake, but the other side was veiled by a shimmering haze. The water looked warm and unhealthy, very different to the water in the pool he'd lingered by earlier. He thought he heard muffled footsteps and the sound of tall grass being brushed aside, but saw no-one.

He spotted the stump of a tree close to the water's edge. He dropped down heavily and stripped off his shirt. He immediately felt better, although the resentment and bitterness, the sense of lost opportunities and being denied them, all of which had accompanied him into the gardens, still smouldered deep inside. He was becoming convinced that he was being observed, if not actually shadowed; a moment later he felt he could just as easily be the pursuer. Vasile let the sun dry his torso and arms. If he got sunburnt it wouldn't matter. Mirela wouldn't be interested, even if he could see her again and tell her. He tried to look at the leaflet that he'd taken, but it was damp and fell apart as he attempted to unfold it. The map was smeared and unreadable. Useless, he stuffed it back into his pocket.

A shadow fell across his face. Startled, Vasile picked up his shirt and dug into the pocket for his sunglasses, but they had gone. At first he thought it was the man he'd encountered in the refreshment room, but then he realised that this man wore a closely trimmed white beard. He was holding a scythe. He smiled at Vasile, and he thought there was a look of recognition.

"You are still here?" the man said.

Vasile's throat was dry. He coughed when he tried to speak. "What do you mean? Do we know each other?"

"I just cut the grass." He made motions with his scythe. "Don't worry, I won't cut you, I've been doing this since I was very young. I enjoy keeping the paths clear and cutting new ones."

"How do you know where to go?"

"I'm allowed to do it my way."

"You looked at me like you'd seen me before. Do you know me?"

He smiled and shook his head. "Clearly not."

"It's hot, isn't it?" Vasile said. "I've never been here before."

"All right."

"I thought I might've seen someone, though." He paused. "Or I felt him."

"I just cut the grass. That's all I do."

The path followed a sinuous stream which flowed into the lake. In the haze Vasile glimpsed someone on the path ahead of him, but when he reached the figure it was a young tree, newly-planted and with a post supporting it. He touched the wood, running his fingers up and down the rough surface. It had been treated with creosote, and the pungent smell brought back memories of when he'd helped his father to repair an old wooden fence and coat it. The anger left him, and then the pain flowed away. Why worry about Mirela? He had done the right thing by not asking her to marry him after all. Someone else could have that pleasure. He'd rather face the future on his own than gain her, be with her, and then lose her.

Vasile looked around him. He blinked several times in quick succession. There it was again: a figure on the curving path behind him. He wondered if he should approach him, or hurry away in the opposite direction, or try to hide in the long grass. To strike out from where he now stood and to leave the place behind would be a great risk. He felt anxious. The sun must be burning the other man's bare skin. He took off his sunglasses and peered into the hot afternoon. Light flooded his senses. It was the man with the scythe, not the other one—and he wasn't on the path, but in the middle of the long grass. He was steadily cutting a swathe through it, on a course taking him towards the lake.

"You still here?" the gardener said when he'd got close enough.

"Do we know each other?"

"I just cut the grass."

Vasile rubbed his finger and thumb together, expectantly, as if the memory of holding an object was still fresh.

"Can I use that way?" He pointed at the path that the man with the scythe had just been cutting.

The man shrugged his shoulders.

Vasile turned abruptly. More sweat broke out from his forehead and trickled down his temples and cheeks, and into his eyes. He started to walk back in the direction of the palace. He put on his damp shirt again and wiped his face with his handkerchief. As he pushed it back into his pocket his fingertips touched his watch and keys. He was sure now that he was alone as he wandered through the gardens. There were no glimpses, no intrusions—not on this path, at least. He knew that he would come back again—and for as many times as it took—just to make sure.

A Gift for the Emperor

The suite of rooms reserved for the Hohenzollern monarchs at the manor house of Ziellenstein was about to be made ready for a new guest. The rooms had been kept permanently available since the Great Elector, Friedrich Wilhelm I, first visited in 1670; and every monarch since had stayed in them at one time or another. Over the generations the monarch's title had changed and expanded, but whether in his august person he was Elector of Brandenburg, Duke of Prussia, King in Prussia, King of Prussia, the German Emperor—or a combination of any number of those titles, shifting with the years—the rooms at Ziellenstein were always available for him, and normally at no more than an hour's notice.

The exterior of Ziellenstein manor house was plain—even austere—as befitted the residence of one of the most important Junker families in the province. As the decades accumulated, the manor house had grown into a medium-sized palace. When viewed from the extensive formal gardens surrounding the house, its white façades projected a firm sense of solidity and permanence: a no-nonsense spirit that was intended both to reassure and make an impression. By way of contrast, all was glorious within. The main halls and rooms ranged in style from the most refined and coolest Greek and Roman through all other varieties of classical to the baroque. The kitchens were finished in an Assyrian style with some genuinely ancient brickwork and tiles; there were Chinoiserie bathrooms and an Egyptian billiard room. The chapel had been refurbished in a gloomy and romantic mock gothic for King Friedrich Wilhelm IV. What Ziellenstein lacked in exterior splendour it also made up for in size, and in consequence was described in some circles as the Versailles of East Prussia.

The current Lord of Ziellenstein, Count Philipp von Stern, was amused by this informal comparison made by some of his fellow landowners as well as many of his guests. But the thought of living in a Prussian Versailles—no matter how magnificent—held no interest for him. For Stern, to compare Ziellenstein to any other palace, no matter how much or little the comparison was deserved, represented a loss of its uniqueness and was not to be dreamed of. And yet there was one comparison that Stern would have been delighted and gratified to have known his friends and guests to make. His unspoken desire was for his country house to be regarded by all as the Sanssouci of East Prussia. In particular, he had spent a considerable amount of time and money on maintaining and enlarging the great library, which now consisted of more than forty thousand volumes, to say nothing of the manuscripts, architectural prints, plans, maps, letters, and various other papers in the family archives.

As he issued final orders for the opening-up of the royal rooms, Stern reflected that his library was effectively an unexplored region for the current Emperor, Wilhelm II. He smiled to himself as he imagined the two entirely separate salons or parties that he could entertain without them ever coming into contact or even learning of each other's existence. Two sets of breakfasts, lunches, and dinners could be served in their respective and different rooms in opposite wings of the house; the gentlemen from each gathering would not have to come into each other's presence before or afterwards either. Nevertheless, Stern was careful to invite his artistic and literary friends to stay only when he did not expect a visit from his King and Emperor.

The Emperor was expected at any moment. Stern had sent his best carriage to the station to meet the Emperor's special train. He'd considered sending his new Mercedes, but as he hadn't been too sure about the Emperor's attitude to motorised transport, even that designed and manufactured in Germany, he had decided against it. He could always put the car at his sovereign's complete disposal during his stay.

Stern strode up to where his butler was standing in the entrance hall.

"No sign yet, Thorsten?" he asked.

"Nothing, My Lord." He took out his watch and glanced at it. "The rooms are ready, and I've no doubt that His Majesty's train arrived at the halt on time."

"Exactly on time."

"Yes, so the carriage should be here very shortly, I'm sure, My Lord."

Stern leaned forward slightly, as if straining to catch the slightest sound penetrating the thick walls of the manor house from outside.

"I believe I hear something. Thorsten, please open the door."

The two men walked out onto the terrace in front of the house and stopped at the top of the steps leading down to the gravel drive. Their breath clouded in the clear glacial air. A carriage was just visible on the far side of the lake, where the drive followed the shore in a wide curve before aiming itself straight at the centre of the main façade of the house.

"Let's go," Stern said, winking at the butler. They walked slowly down the steps, timing themselves so they reached the bottom just as the carriage drew up. Thorsten moved forward and opened the gilt-encrusted door with a white-gloved hand. Stern prepared himself to help the Emperor down the steps of the carriage and to bow before being offered the imperial hand. They waited in front of the open door as the seconds ticked away.

"Get a move on," Thorsten whispered.

"Your Majesty . . . ?" Stern said. He mounted the first step up into the carriage, and began to put his head around the open door and into the dark interior.

"It's empty," the coachman shouted down. "The Emperor ain't in there. He didn't turn up!"

Stern fell back as if he'd been pushed out of the carriage by an invisible hand. He beckoned to the coachman to come down. Thorsten went to take hold of the reins.

"What are you talking about, Ernst?" Stern asked.

"What I said. I got to the station in plenty of time like you ordered, My Lord, and waited for the train. It came in dead on time, and they're all lined up on the platform to meet the train. Well, the door opens and a man gets out. He's wearing a uniform, all gold and stuff. He ain't our Emperor, I think to myself. He's one of the monkeys and not the organ-grinder, and I saw him last time he was here. This man says something to the stationmaster, who gets into the compartment. I thought His Majesty had fallen asleep, maybe. Then the stationmaster gets out again, and he and the gent in the uniform are carrying this big flat parcel. They bring it over to where I'm waiting and tell me to put it in the carriage. It's in there now. And he gave me a letter. For you, sir. Here."

The coachman held out an envelope. Stern took it, and noticed the imperial monogram embossed on the front in gold. He tucked the envelope into a pocket and climbed up into the carriage. As the coachman had said, there was a large flat object propped up on the seat, where a passenger would be. It was a parcel wrapped in brown paper, tied with gold-coloured cord and studded with several royal and imperial seals in different coloured waxes.

"If this is one of his practical jokes . . . " he muttered to himself.

The parcel had been unwrapped and stood up against a tall bookcase in the library. Stern, his wife, and the butler stood in front of it. Stern held the letter that had accompanied it.

"Let me read that," Countess von Stern said.

"Certainly, Gisela."

"Thank you. Let's see. Blah blah blah, the usual, We this, Our that, My the other, blah blah blah. Ha! Something's come up at the Court at Potsdam, he can't come here as planned, but sends a modest gift to make up for it. Well, Philipp, I've never seen a gift from a member of our Royal Family quite like this one. And the von Sterns have received enough Hohenzollern gifts over the centuries to fill a museum. At any rate, we'll still be in his presence. Well, well. A nice big painting of Wilhelm— from Wilhelm. And I should think that it's unique!"

"Why should it be unique, my dear?" the Count asked. "There are a great number of portraits of the Emperor."

"Yes, but I'm very sure that it's the only painting of him I've seen where he's not wearing one of those bloody stupid ornate uniforms he adores. Even if he does pose like a tailor's dummy in that nice English tweed suit! And holding a book like that instead of a gun or a sword doesn't fool anyone. Philipp, the good thing is that there won't now be the usual slaughter of animal life on the estate!"

"Until the next time," Stern said. "And while we think of it we had better decide where to hang that picture. He'll look for it, mark my words. We'll never hear the end of it if it's not prominent or not prominent enough!"

"Might I suggest that it's hung in here, My Lord?" Thorsten said. "If the portrait of your great-grandfather is moved a little to the left, the Emperor's new portrait will fit in quite nicely, I think. The frames would match rather well. And the painting would be clearly seen. I could get some of the men onto it straight away, if you're agreeable, sir."

The Count and Countess agreed, and the Emperor's gift was duly hung in its new setting.

That evening after dinner the Count wandered into the library and stood in front of the portrait. As in every other portrait of Wilhelm II that Stern had seen, he glared out at the beholders he always seemed to be so certain were there. The ends of his moustache were waxed to perfection and stood at rigid attention, and he held the book with a manifestly strong grip, as if it was hard-won and not to be let go without a struggle. Stern met the Emperor's truculent gaze. He felt rooted to the spot, as if he really were in the imperial presence. He ran his hand over his closely-cropped beard and let it remain there cupping his chin. A few minutes later the Countess joined him. She touched his arm gently and smiled.

"Has that man mesmerised you?"

Stern shook his head to clear away his thoughts. "Something's not right," he told her. "We haven't had a portrait as a gift since Friedrich Wilhelm II gave us his in 1788. They usually give us a silver tankard or a vase or something like that. Not a portrait. Now it's like having him here. I keep expecting him to step into the room and give me an order. It's positively eerie. And there's a reason for it, I'm sure."

"It's the civilian clothes," the Countess said.

"It's the book," the Count replied.

"Has he ever read a book while staying here?"

Stern thought for a moment. He had never heard anything to contradict the view that the Emperor never glanced at a book unless it concerned military or naval matters, was a royal biography, or a novel in English by a popular author such as Scott, Dickens, or Twain. It was said that Goethe's *Faust* was also in his repertoire. And he would only open a book when the weather was so bad that there could not be even the slightest possibility of any hunting. The Count now told his wife that he remembered that on one occasion during his last visit the Emperor had admitted to enjoying the verse of Rudyard Kipling. After dinner he had asked for a volume to be brought to him from the library and then recited several poems, word-perfect, while his fellow guests, mainly courtiers roughing it in the wilds of East Prussia with their lord and master, had looked on with the proper expressions of admiration. Upon retiring for the night the Emperor had taken the book to his room, and kept it until his departure.

"Yes, you're right, Philipp," his wife said. "I recall that as well, now. I don't care much for Kipling." She peered at the portrait. "Are you thinking what I'm thinking?"

They walked over to one of the baroque bookcases. "Let's see," the Countess said. They searched the shelves.

"Yes, here we are. Kipling." She reached up and pulled out the volume, and walked back over to the portrait of the Emperor.

"Now he seems to be looking at me and the book at the same time," Stern said.

They examined the volume of Kipling, and then the book in the Emperor's hand. The Countess held up the real book against the painted one.

"Identical! Wilhelm's holding the Ziellenstein copy of Kipling!"

Stern yawned and rubbed his eyes. His wife poured out a cup of coffee and passed it to him.

"I hardly slept at all," he said. "I couldn't stop thinking about that portrait and the Kipling book. There's a definite reason for Wilhelm sending that picture, I just know it. There was nothing special about the book that I could see, and yet it must have significance. He's up to something, even if it's yet another one of his jokes."

"Have some more coffee," the Countess said. "One would think he would have better things to do. He has an empire to run, or interfere in, for a start."

"My dear! Not when the servants could hear—"

"Hoh! Sometimes they and people like them know the truth better than we do. They see through it all, including Wilhelm King and Emperor at the top of the pile. The trouble is that man's just never really grown up. If he were only the buffoon or clown he so often looks and acts it would be bad enough, although not all bad. We could put up with that. He could be contained. But as it is he could lead the country into serious danger. Who knows what he could do in the future, even if he doesn't mean to, or doesn't realise the consequences of his actions and speeches? England is worried, and that isn't good, is it? If only he hadn't got rid of Bismarck! I still miss the Iron Chancellor, even though he's been dead for well over ten years!"

"Gisela, I hadn't realised you took such an interest in political and military affairs," the Count said. He lowered his voice. "But I have to say that I fear you may be right. Wilhelm pays these visits, as when he went to Tangier. He does things such as sending that gunboat to Agadir. And millions of marks are poured away like water into our so-called colonies. A place in the sun, he says! Ha, don't get me started. But I was saying that Wilhelm's up to something. If only I could put my finger on it. Well, I'll get out into the fresh air today and try to forget about it all. Perhaps I will do a little hunting."

"Well—good luck. 'True friends whom I so oft have found, Say, for our scheme on German ground, What prospect have we of success?' "

"What was that?"

"Goethe, my dear Philipp. *Faust*."

The Count spent most of the day strolling around the parts of the Ziellenstein estate that lay within a few kilometres of the manor house. He had decided not to take a gun with him: the Emperor's cancellation—or, more likely, postponement—of his visit had granted a stay of execution to the wildlife of his land which Stern didn't wish to revoke even to the smallest extent. The exercise revived him. Despite the sleeplessness of the previous night and the lurking sense of foreboding that had clung to him since his conversation with the Countess at breakfast, Stern's spirits had risen. It was a chilly but sunny day, with small white clouds scudding across the limitless blue sky. Frost rimed the grass where it remained in shadow. Whenever Stern stopped and stared, the only boundary to his outlook was the horizon. The meadows and stretches of forest he tramped through, the streams he crossed and lakes he walked around: all refreshed him as he reacquainted himself with them. It was like visiting the estate of a beloved friend after a long absence, rather than his own land: things familiar to him were as new. Stern greeted and spoke to everyone he met: all were workers on his estate, tenants or contracted employees, and relied on him for their livelihoods. Resting by the canal he watched a boat transporting a load of freshly-felled timber to the sawmill that his grandfather had built. Hours later, as he trudged back towards the great house, its long white façade glowing orange in the setting sun, Stern remembered his wife's words from breakfast.

A servant helped him out of his heavy coat, and told him that Thorsten had ordered a bath to be prepared, which would now be ready. As he soaked gratefully in the hot soapy water, Stern contemplated the day he had spent out and about on his land. The Emperor might be able to do as he liked, but Count Philipp von Stern of Ziellenstein had responsibilities.

The Count was smiling as he took his place opposite his wife at dinner.

"I've been thinking a bit more," the Countess said.

"Yes, Gisela?"

"About that painting."

"Ah, what else?"

"I am sorry to spoil things. I know you had a good day. But the fact remains."

"Yes."

"You said you thought Wilhelm had a reason for sending that picture, and there was almost certainly a meaning contained in it, as well."

"Correct."

"It occurred to me that although Wilhelm can be so devious on occasion, here he's being totally obvious. It is the book, isn't it? As you said. Kipling. Philipp, you know as well as I do what a man like Wilhelm would do if he wanted something. Why, he'd send a gift first, wouldn't he? Although he'd die sooner than admit it, the Emperor thinks of himself as something of an *arriviste*, somewhat inferior, and is always trying to compensate. And he's so volatile. Worst of all, he projects all of that onto the country. You and I know that he is far from being ill-bred, but one might sometimes wonder. He can so often come over as an ill-mannered lout and virtually a philistine. Yet he quoted all those Kipling poems and took the book to his room. Something about that book is important to him. The Emperor is ordering us to give him that book— as a present! I only wish I knew exactly what is so vital, why he must have it."

"Well, a poem, surely?"

The Countess nodded, and sipped her wine. "I thought to myself that it would be useful if we could remember what the Emperor read out to us that night. I've tried but I just can't remember. But I thought you might be able to, Philipp. That might cast some light on all this, don't you think?"

"You may well have something there, my love," he said after a few minutes had passed. "But I can't remember the poems he read. I don't have that sort of memory."

The butler stepped forward. "My Lord?"

"What is it, Thorsten?"

"I beg your pardon, but I did hear . . . You know I never reveal anything, but this time I think I should say . . . My Lord, I am certain that I can tell you which poems the Emperor recited. My English is not at all bad, and I was there. Yes, I remember perfectly."

Stern laughed. "Your memory must be as good as Wilhelm's! That's to say, His Majesty's! Excellent. Very well, please go and write down the titles and the Countess and I will go through the list in the library after dinner. We really are most grateful to you, Thorsten."

"Oh, and Thorsten, put the book out as well, please," the Countess added.

Thorsten finished writing out the list of poems. He folded the sheet once and slid it into a plain white envelope, which he sealed. He had already removed the book from its place on the shelves and left it in the middle of the table nearest to where the Count and Countess would sit to drink their coffee. The butler walked at a stately pace back to the library, and he was just in time to open the door for his master and mistress. They sat down and Thorsten gestured to the waiting servant to pour the coffee. He took the envelope from his pocket.

"Thorsten, have you prepared that list?" Stern asked. "Ah, I see you have. Now, this is no time for ceremony. Please sit down here and join us for coffee. Are your duties able to spare you for a few minutes?"

"My Lord, I am honoured. Shall I get the book?"

"No!" the Countess said sharply. "I'm sorry—I did not mean to startle anyone. No, Thorsten, please leave it where it is, at least for the present. But do sit down. Have some coffee."

Stern was about to tear open the envelope when his wife leaned over and stopped him. "Philipp, wait for a moment." She pinched an edge of the envelope between thumb and forefinger. "Don't open it. Here, let me have it for now."

The Count gave her a quizzical look, and let her pluck the envelope from his hand.

"I've been giving this matter much more thought," the Countess said. "Thorsten, please tell me and the Count what, if anything, you saw in the Emperor's rooms during his visit. What I mean is: did you see the book of poems? Was the Emperor doing anything with it?"

"My Lady . . . "

"It's all right, Thorsten. Anything you say will go no further than we three here. I guarantee it. We know the Emperor trusts us all when he is our guest, and I assure you that he will have no reason to change his mind. So you may speak freely."

The butler drank some coffee. "Well, later that evening His Majesty rang and asked for a glass of Scotch whisky. I decided to take it up to him myself. Before I knocked at the door I could hear His Majesty's voice, as if he were reading out loud to an audience. I thought he was reciting another one of those English poems. I was sure the Emperor was pacing around the room, because his voice kept getting louder then quieter. But when I went in I saw His Majesty sitting at the desk in the lounge. He looked like he'd rushed there just a moment before. The poetry book was open on the desk. The desk was covered with papers, and His Majesty picked up some dispatches that had been delivered by special courier earlier in the day. There were pens and pencils all over the place, and the Emperor wrote things on the papers while I was there. I also think he'd been making notes in the book. There was a pencil resting on the open pages. His Majesty closed the book just as I got to where he was sitting to give him his glass of whisky. But I couldn't actually make out any words or underlinings, anything like that."

"I see," Stern said. "And what were the dispatches? Could you tell?"

"All I know is that they were from the General Staff. By the look of them I assumed from Field Marshal von Schlieffen himself."

The Count looked up with a start.

"I mean the late Field Marshal's successor, of course, My Lord."

"Have you examined the book, Thorsten?" the Countess said. "I mean, closely."

He shook his head.

"Very well, Thorsten, thank you. And now please take your time and finish your coffee, and then you may leave us."

The lamps had been turned down low, but the fire still burned bright, filling the library with a fantasia of flickering and shadows. Darkness and cold pressed in from the corners of the immense room. Stern rang the bell and asked for two large glasses of cognac.

"I still don't want anyone to open that book," the Countess said.

"And there are definitely no pieces of paper, photographs, or anything like that in it, are there?"

"Very unlikely, I'd say. I think we'd have been able to tell. They would most likely have fallen out."

"And the Emperor's annotations or notes . . . "

"We've been through this," said the Countess. "As far as I can tell there's only a possibility that there were annotations or notes. And so there's a possibility that there were none at all. Are some: are none at all."

"My dear, the matter is easily resolved. I think we should simply send him the book. It can go tomorrow. Let's just give the Emperor what he so clearly wants from us. My family has always been obedient. The Sterns of Ziellenstein have always done the bidding of their monarch; our home and all it contains has always been at their disposal." He gazed balefully at the book, still lying on the table where the butler had left it. "All this intrigue caused by a book of English poems," he murmured. "Is there really anything to all this, I wonder?"

The cognac arrived. "Please ask Mr. Thorsten to come," the Countess said to the servant.

The Count pointed at the book. "Thorsten, please take that volume and wrap it up well and securely. Find a suitable container for it—perhaps one of those silver boxes in the South Corridor might be appropriate. I will make the arrangements to have it sent to the Emperor in the morning. And now please take it out of our sight."

"My Lord."

The Countess spoke. "Thorsten, the Count and I would prefer it if you kept the book shut. Please do not open it or let anyone else open it. Wrap it up straight away and seal the package, so nobody but His Majesty can open it. We will write a letter to go with this gift. It will be ready first thing in the morning."

"I think you said the right thing, as usual," the Count told his wife when they were alone once more. "Thorsten's no fool. His family has been with us about as long as we've been here at Ziellenstein. He feels something, just as we do."

"I wish the Emperor felt something. Why is he putting us through this test? Doesn't he think we won't open the book to have a look before sending it to him? And why shouldn't we? What difference would it make?"

"And that's why we've been right to resist that temptation," Stern replied. "I just know that if we go through the book, if we tried to find out what the Emperor wrote in it, why and in what connection, that very act could change things. I've never felt such a sense of apprehension and threat. And the thought of anything to do with old Schlieffen fills me with worry." He gazed into the fire. "I see it in those flames: changes are on their way that could engulf us all and eventually sweep away Ziellenstein together with everything we've built and everyone we love and care for. I only hope Wilhelm knows what he wants with his gift and what to do when he gets it. But to trust to that . . . I don't know, my dear Gisela, I really don't know."

The Count got up from his chair. He knelt down next to where his wife was sitting and took her hands in his. He kissed them. Then he released her hands and opened his palm. She laid the sealed envelope in it and shook her head.

"Would you even think it, Philipp?"

Stern walked over to the fireplace and stoked the fire blazing there. Then he thrust the envelope into the very heart of the mass of flames.

The Count and Countess finished their breakfast in silence. Stern had approved Thorsten's choice of a container for the book: a wooden box inlaid with Samland amber and fitted with an engraved silver lock. The Count himself had turned the key in the lock, before in turn sealing it inside an envelope bearing the Ziellenstein crest. Then he had laid it on top of the box and directed Thorsten to wrap it there and then. The Countess applied the wax seals. As she did so her expression remained impassive; unreadable even to her husband.

"Now please send the carriage to the station again," the Count told his butler. "I have the feeling that a special train will be waiting. The things one has to do in order to provide a gift for the Emperor."

Into an Empire

Payton liked to leave his house at sunset in order to post orders for the coins, banknotes, and postage stamps he wished to buy for his collection. Although he only collected those from a small range of countries and specific periods of their history, he was nonetheless attracted to any items that aroused his curiosity or eye for beauty and good design. These criteria, rather than any intrinsic value, were what he cherished: things that had (or could have had) an interesting story behind them, or seemed to him to symbolise or sum up an event or an age. The vanished empires of Central and Eastern Europe held a special fascination for him—a persistent glamour. Payton pored over atlases and maps, following the shifting lines of frontiers and the shuffling of entire lands as marked by the ebb and flow of expanses of colour across the page. He learned that what may seem to be permanent at the time never really is—empires certainly not excepted. Whether an empire which had slowly come together over centuries or one that had suddenly arrived new-born through the blood of soldiers and subjects and the signatures of statesmen—it could vanish, seemingly without trace.

Inevitably Payton absorbed himself in the eras of great instability and turmoil. In particular this meant the three decades or so between the beginning of the First World War and the ending of the Second. The empires of Austria-

Hungary, Germany, and Russia had been wiped off the map, and the number of those who remembered them from experience grew daily fewer. When he meditated on the contents of his collection he felt the touch of the gross uncertainty that had prevailed, especially during episodes of scarcity and hyperinflation. When metal money had vanished and trust in paper worn out as the savings and dignity of millions went with it, the world had rocked on its new and shallow foundations. There had been no security or solid place to stand and be safe—to contemplate or simply to be. Payton's own contemplations sometimes led him into a subdued terror at the prospect of that world reviving itself and reaching back to engulf his. For him the void left by the empires' passing never ceased gaping; and so it was tangible remnants of the vanished realms—coins in particular—that he loved to collect. He came to feel that his accumulation of them was to maintain more than a vital memory; perhaps it was even to practice a form of redemption. He sought his own peace and security through his interests and the routines that grew into place surrounding and sustaining them.

Payton spoke to no one about his interests; neighbours and work colleagues had no idea how he spent his earnings. He never visited dealers—even those whom he had dealt with for many years, and knew his wishes exactly—despite the fact many of them were in the West End or Bloomsbury, a journey away by Tube. Payton had the conviction that to actually meet one of his suppliers, or to enter their premises in person, would somehow unbalance things and lead to unforeseen and far-reaching consequences. Once Payton had been travelling on a bus as it slowly threaded its way between the various Finchleys and Barnets when he realised with dismay it was about to pass the shop from where he had recently ordered some ten and twenty crown pieces from pre-Munich Czechoslovakia. Only just managing to conceal his panic he had rushed downstairs and sat gazing at the grimy floor until he knew there could no longer be any chance of catching a glimpse of the shop. While he had no doubt that the dealers he corresponded with were fine and friendly people, and his relations with them were unfailingly cordial, he conducted his business exclusively through the post.

Turnham Park, where Payton lived in a small house bought with the proceeds of his parents' estate, was well provided with pillar boxes. He had adopted the routine of posting his orders in specific boxes, and could no longer conceive of any other system. He could not justify to himself why he had to use a particular pillar box for orders for particular items; it just had to be. Orders to one dealer went in the box at the end of his road; orders to another in the box built into the wall outside the post office by The Green. All orders for banknotes were posted in the pillar box on the side of the railway bridge nearest the High Road. He would split orders to the same dealer if it included items for which he would otherwise have used different pillar boxes: an order for German hyperinflation postage stamps had to go from the box at the corner of Truman Row and Voysey Avenue, while silver five mark coins bearing the square profile of President Hindenburg from the same catalogue could only be ordered by using a pillar box situated on the edge of the suburb close to Chiswick Park Tube station.

So Payton developed a complex web of routes between the pillar boxes he had to use. To him each had its own characteristics, not least because of the royal cypher it carried. He wondered whether that had influenced his choice, but had never worked out any connections that made sense, although nebulous patterns did sometimes seem to be a possibility. It was clear that orders for items from the Austro-Hungarian Empire always had to go through certain pillar boxes bearing the graceful interlocking curves and arcs of Queen Victoria's cypher or the more intricate and ornate one of Edward VII, but not George VI's agreeable and relaxed cypher. This rule did not apply to the Empire's successor states except for Austria itself: a set of aluminium coins from Hungary struck towards the end of Admiral Horthy's regency had to be ordered using a pillar box bearing the solid and impassive GR of King George V.

As the daylight drained from the sky, Turnham Park seemed more than ever a place somehow not quite connected with the rest of the sprawling mass of London; in the dusk the suburb gave the impression of not being quite on the same plane or fully sharing in a common geography. During the winter, night fell while Payton returned from work. The sky over the suburb would be a pale and frosty blue, almost white in its intensity, with bare trees silhouetted against the violet and lemon afterglow, and mountainous clouds as flaming as if from one of Turner's more apocalyptic scenes. Payton walked from the bus stop in the High Road by the brightly-lit shopping parade and on his way home visited as many of the pillar boxes as was necessary. Payton enjoyed his extended evening walks, although he often did not arrive back at his house until well after dark.

In summer the afterglow lingered long and late. Payton strolled past the dark bulk of garden hedges and red brick houses luminous and with their white rendering glowing in the reflected light of sunset, returning the day's heat into the gathering lavender-scented dusk. And in autumn, the suburb's tall chimneys, its gables and rooftops were etched against the flaring reds and oranges of the west, while molten smears of cloud overhead still held gold from the sun. It was at the times when the seasons were in flux that Payton sensed, more than ever, a singular kinship with the place where he lived, and which included the objects he collected, their stories and the lost places from which they had made their way to him.

It was an evening in late August. The windows of the house glimmered in the twilight and threw faint panels of lamplight into the garden. Payton glanced out one more time before he methodically went from room to room closing all the curtains. Moments later his short, slim, neat, figure quickly emerged from the house, slamming the front door behind him as if to give warning of his presence to the street outside. He patted the pockets of his jacket and drew out a number of small white envelopes. He counted them and replaced them, before running his hands over his short black hair and stepping gently on to the brick-paved path that led to the gate in the low white wooden fence and the suburb beyond.

At the end of his street Payton crossed the road diagonally and stopped by the pillar box there, its Edward VII cypher prominent once more under its blazing coat of new paint. After making sure he was unobserved, he bent down and ran his fingers over and around its smooth curves and coils as if performing a ceremony or weaving a signal as elaborate as his course through the streets of Turnham Park. There was a flicker of white as he posted an envelope into the slot, hearing it drop with a stifled rustling on top of the items already inside. He then strolled along, taking the second turning left and then right. The next pillar box was built into the sturdy brick corner pier of the garden wall surrounding one of the large and gracious detached houses that Payton had always coveted—some of the first built when Turnham Park had been opened to development. The tall windows and steep roof of the house rose up against the deepening blue sky; the windows of the little cupola floating above the dormers reflected the moon as it drifted out from behind a thin banner of cloud. Payton dropped two envelopes into the box and continued walking.

Streetlamps marched into the darkness on either side, heads bowing to the inky sky and the pervasive glow of London. He passed two pillar boxes, touching each lightly as he did so to assure it that it was not forgotten, just not to be called upon to serve this evening. In the George V box at the end of another street he posted another order. Payton now stood with The Green spread out in front of him. The grass had been cut; its fragrance suddenly banished time and filled him with yearning. Light and clamour poured from the open doors and windows of the Park Tavern. Payton dug his hands into his pockets, feeling the two remaining envelopes there. He strode across The Green, keeping to one of the straight tarmac paths cutting through the damp grass.

The penultimate envelope slid out of sight. The route to the last pillar box lay at the far end of his favourite stretch of road in Turnham Park: a street lined on both sides by great old trees that formed a virtual tunnel. Their branches arched and met above the road: a network of cracks in the sky in winter and a shadowy and mystery-filled passage in summer. The very last of the light was draining from the sky as Payton passed under the first pair of trees. It was warm and close in the darkness. Streetlights sparkled behind the gently waving leaves and car headlights shone into Payton's eyes. The street ahead beyond the far end of the tunnel was barely any lighter now than among the trees.

Payton drew the last envelope out of his pocket. Normally he would post it without even looking. He knew what the order was for and where it was going; therefore he was posting it in the correct pillar box. As the envelope dropped out of view he saw the address pre-printed in heavy black type: the dealer always enclosed a postage paid envelope with his catalogues and order forms. It was not the order it should have been. He grabbed at the envelope, but met only air before his knuckles grazed the lip of the slot in a jolt of pain. The envelope landed with a quiet sigh. It should have been posted in the previous pillar box.

He reached out and laid his hand on the cold and clammy metal as he thought about what had happened; the error he had made. For a moment Payton considered trying to force his arm into the mouth of the pillar box, but he dismissed the idea straight away. He could return in the morning and attempt to catch the postman emptying the box, and ask for his order back; but as he imagined himself pleading for its return he knew he would be refused. And he would have to go through the whole process again with the other order lying in the other box. If he waited in vigil all night until the postman came, it would surely make no difference. What if the mistake had occurred far back towards the beginning of his route? Perhaps he had posted most or all of his orders in the wrong pillar boxes. He could not go back and change things, to undo all that he had done. Payton turned away and began to walk home, sick at heart at what he had allowed himself to do.

Over the years Payton had taken to arranging small piles of coins, like tiny ziggurats, on certain shelves or on top of some of his many bookcases. On sunny windowsills or in other places he set out a number of small, shallow bowls and dishes, and left coins in those, arranged so they touched each other and covered the maximum area of surface without overlapping. He chose silver, brass, aluminium, and copper coins, laying them down in patterns and combinations without really knowing why he did it. It was as if he were leaving offerings to an unknown divinity, force, or motive. Yet whatever the reason, to him his careful actions had an obscure inspiration, and left him with a sense of order and calm.

When he got back home he switched on a single light and sat down in an armchair and stared at a small dish of silver coins from 1920s Latvia set out on the low table in front of him. Against the deep green of the glazed pottery holding them, the lustre of the coins filled the dish like the unbroken surface of water. In the shadow-filled room specks of silver light glinted on the walls. He soon felt rather more in possession of himself. As midnight approached Payton had come to the conclusion that whatever he had done, his orders should still be delivered to the right places. No matter what he thought, the postal authorities would have no interest whatsoever in which pillar boxes he used. In the morning he would resume his routines and go to work as usual, and await his deliveries.

During the next few evenings, although he posted no new orders, Payton still left his house at sunset and wandered the hushed streets of Turnham Park as dusk advanced into night. Everything presented the appearance of regularity: low-angled orange light flooding over grass, trees, and houses; the swollen September moon sailing up over The Green; the streetlights on parade and the Tube trains clattering along their embankment; the faint kiss of ground frost hinting of the bite autumn would have in store for the bright crispness of the morning.

The coins and banknotes Payton had ordered began to arrive within the week. As he picked up the padded envelopes from the doormat he was reassured by this further sign of normality, and its vindication of his rationalisations on the night he had come to think of as a sort of fall from grace. As he tipped the packets out on to the table, he noted that the correct items had been sent by the correct dealers. Payton took the catalogues from the cupboard and started to check what he had ordered against what was in front of him. It was then he realised something was different after all. He had ordered an Austrian silver two schilling piece from 1934, struck only in that year to commemorate Dr. Dollfuss. It had been offered graded extremely fine, rather than the uncirculated he would have preferred had it been available. But as he examined the coin he realised that what he held was in proof condition, and so rare indeed—and expensive. He examined the other items that had been delivered. There was a five billion mark note from Germany, in perfect crisp uncirculated, much better grade than advertised. Another packet contained a silver five liati piece from Lithuania that had only been available with considerable toning. The coin he actually held seemed freshly minted, polished and shining. Payton put the coins away, thinking he would have to write to the dealers and inform them of their costly mistakes.

It was when Payton got home from work the following evening that he received the greatest surprise of all. He had ordered a batch of German hyperinflation covers: complete envelopes plastered with colourful mosaics of postage stamps to the value of millions of marks. And there they were, littering the floor of the hall as if they had just been pushed through the letterbox. His first reaction was one of annoyance: the envelope and protective wrapping that the dealer invariably used had clearly been torn away. He carefully picked up the scattered envelopes, but there was no sign of any outer packaging. The covers were as clean as they could have been after making a single journey through the post; the envelopes seemed to have come straight from the stationer's and the stamps just torn from the sheet on the post office clerk's counter. The postmarks were not smudged; neither were the sharp strokes of the sender's handwriting—although he couldn't read a word of it due to the particular style of script. Payton carried the covers through to his sitting room and placed them on the table next to the dish of coins. He went through the envelopes, turning them over one by one. They were still sealed and held their contents; he had no wish to open them and see what was inside. He dropped them on the table and sat back in his armchair.

Payton's letters to his dealers remained unwritten, and their new catalogues unopened. He moved through the warm October days in a reverie, going to work as usual and wandering around Turnham Park in the increasingly cool evenings. He now regarded the pillar boxes as he would any feature he passed in the street. He started to conclude his circuits of the streets with a glass of whisky at the Park Tavern. At home he sometimes absent-mindedly disturbed the contents of one of his dishes of coins or unintentionally knocked over one of the small piles; but he left them in their new positions or where they had been scattered.

As autumn wore on, the time Payton got off the bus coincided with nightfall. The sunset painted the bulky brick buildings of the High Road and illuminated the yellow and gold of the trees. He strolled home through fallen leaves littering The Green and layering the pavements, feeling the bite of the damp chill air against his face. Houses caught the fires of sunset in their windows as he chose routes that kept the last of the sun and afterglow in sight until the light faded away behind the rooftops. He persisted in following the paths between pillar boxes, pleased each time to see them still there, faithfully in place even as the year waned and he had no more use for them.

And every evening Payton walked through the tunnel of trees towards the glow of sunset. Now at last he dreamed, not of emerging at the far end but instead coming to the other side of the dying fires, of joining and becoming one with an empire which had never ceased to exist, even though its tokens littered the world.

Sources

My thanks to Eoin Llewellyn for the use of his artwork, and to the following editors and publishers for the first appearances of these stories, as follows:

" 'Where Once I Did My Love Beguile' "
was first published in *Beneath the Ground*, edited by Joel Lane. Alchemy Press, 2003.

"Silver on Green"
was first published in *This Hermetic Legislature: A Homage to Bruno Schulz*, edited by D.T. Ghetu. Ex Occidente Press, 2012.

"Winter's Traces"
was first published in *The First Book of Classical Horror Stories*, edited by D.F. Lewis. Megazanthus Press 2012.

"Out to Sea"
was first published in *The Touch of the Sea*, edited by Steve Berman. Lethe Press, 2012.

"Time and the City"
was first published in *The Alchemy Press Book of Ancient Wonders*, edited by Jenny Barber and Jan Edwards. Alchemy Press, 2012.

171

About the Author

John Howard was born in London. His books include *The Silver Voices*, *Written by Daylight*, *Buried Shadows*, *A Flowering Wound*, and *The Voice of the Air*. With Mark Valentine has written the joint collections *Secret Europe*, *Inner Europe*, *Powers and Presences*, and *This World and That Other*. His stories have appeared in many anthologies. He has published essays on various aspects of the science fiction and horror fields, including such iconic authors as Fritz Leiber, Arthur Machen, and August Derleth. He has also written about many now lesser-known and unfairly obscure authors and their work.

SWAN RIVER PRESS

Founded in 2003, Swan River Press is an independent publishing company, based in Dublin, Ireland, dedicated to gothic, supernatural, and fantastic literature. We specialise in limited edition hardbacks, publishing fiction from around the world with an emphasis on Ireland's contributions to the genre.

www.swanriverpress.ie

"While small publishers often produce beautiful books, few can match those from Swan River Press."

– Washington Post

"It [is] often down to small, independent, specialist presses to keep the candle of horror fiction flickering . . ."

– The Irish Times

"Swan River Press—cutting edge of New Gothic."

– Joyce Carol Oates

"The redoubtable Brian J. Showers [keeps] the myriad voices of Irish fantasy alive there in Dublin."

– Alan Moore

THE SILVER VOICES

John Howard

Transylvania: the country beyond the forest and land of the seven fortress towns. In *The Silver Voices* we encounter the previously unknown eighth town: Sternbergstadt. Now known as Steaua de Munte, it's one of those places where past and present continually meet, with no-one being entirely sure which has the upper hand. In Steaua de Munte history can never be said to be dead and buried; it plays too many tricks on the present and future for that.

"Sad . . . with an elegiac quality commemorating all that was lost to the war, the ways in which the world changed for better and worse."

– Black Static

"Ambiguity does not stop with the work's overall composition but proceeds to infect each of the stories . . . Such is the hallmark of gifted writing."

– Dead Reckonings

A FLOWERING WOUND

John Howard

Two of the stories in this collection by John Howard have their setting in a certain west London suburb—the calm prospect of its small houses and tree-lined roads is deceptive. And throughout this selection of stories, whether in outer London or hyperinflationary Berlin, Romania in the febrile 1930s, or the austerity Britain of recent years, we encounter people who live on the peripheries of their cities and societies—and at the edge of their own lives and illusions. They might think they know the rules, but it often turns out they do not, after all. Or perhaps the rules changed—silently, abruptly. In these stories past and present come together with wounding consequences for those caught out by the system—or its absence.

"Some stories recall Arthur Machen's approach to London, his insistence that the great metropolis is a place of magic and mystery."

– Supernatural Tales

"Full of haunting stories of love and confusion . . . a very suitable accompaniment to these terrifying times."

– A Ghostly Company

SEVENTEEN STORIES

Mark Valentine

Mark Valentine's stories have been described by critic Rick Kleffel as "consistently amazing and inexplicably beautiful". He has been called "A superb writer, among the leading practitioners of classic supernatural fiction" by Michael Dirda of the *Washington Post*, and his work is regularly chosen for year's best and other anthologies.

This selection offers previously uncollected or hard to find tales in the finest traditions of the strange and fantastic. As well as tributes to the masters of the field, Valentine provides his own original and otherworldly visions, with what Supernatural Tales has called "the author's trademark erudition" in "unusual byways of history, folklore and general scholarship". Opening a book will never seem quite the same again after encountering this curious volume of *Seventeen Stories* . . .

"Valentine is a writer in love with
the great tradition of the weird tale."

– Supernatural Tales

"[Valentine's] is attentive to place and to the power of
obsession, but one of his true gifts is an ability
to suggest modes of artistic expression."

– The Endless Bookshelf